The Complete FREDDY THE PIG Series
Available from the Overlook Press

FREDDY

and the

MEN *from* MARS

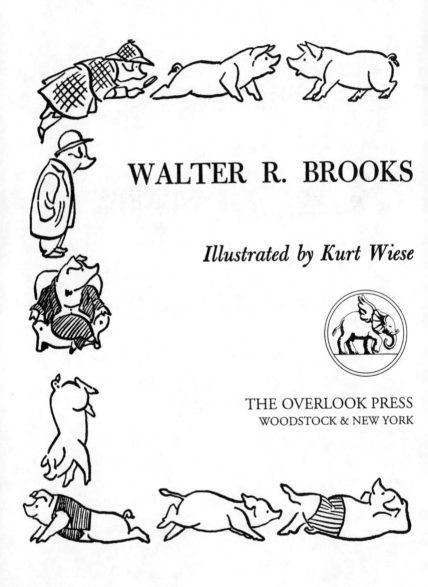

WALTER R. BROOKS

Illustrated by Kurt Wiese

THE OVERLOOK PRESS
WOODSTOCK & NEW YORK

FREDDY

and the

MEN *from* MARS

If you enjoyed this book, very likely you will be interested not only in the other Freddy books published in this series, but also in joining the *Friends of Freddy,* an organization of Freddy devotees.

We will be pleased to hear from any reader about our "Freddy" publishing program. You can easily contact us by logging on the either THE OVERLOOK PRESS website, or the Freddy website.

The website addresses are as follows:
THE OVERLOOK PRESS:
www.overlookpress.com

FREDDY:
www.friendsoffreddy.org

We look forward to hearing from you soon.

First published in the United States in 2002 by
The Overlook Press, Peter Mayer Publishers, Inc.
Woodstock & New York

WOODSTOCK:
One Overlook Drive
Woodstock, NY 12498
www.overlookpress.com
[for individual orders, bulk and special sales, contact our Woodstock office]

NEW YORK:
141 Wooster Street
New York, NY 10012

∞ The paper used in this book meets the requirements for paper permanence as described in the ANSI Z39.48-1992 standard.

Dust jacket and endpaper artwork courtesy of the Lee Secrest collection and archive.

Cataloging-in-Publication Data is available from the Library of Congress

Brooks, Walter R., 1886-1958.
Freddy and the men from Mars / Walter R. Brooks ; illustrated by Kurt Wiese.
p. cm.

Manufactured in the United States of America
ISBN 1-58567-269-6
1 3 5 7 9 8 6 4 2

FOR *Dottie*

FREDDY

and the

MEN *from* MARS

CHAPTER

1

If you went up from the barnyard through the pasture, and past the duck pond, following the brook up into the woods, you came to a road. And if you crossed the road, which was the northern boundary of the Bean farm, pretty soon you were walking among the charred stumps where last year's forest fire had burned over nearly half of the Big Woods. And then right in the middle of the burned area you would have seen a strange thing—a big rocket nearly thirty feet tall, standing on three legs and pointing at the sky.

The rocket looked like pictures you have seen of space ships, built for taking trips to the moon and to other planets, and indeed that is exactly what it was. It had been built by Mr. Bean's Uncle Ben, who was a fine mechanic; and in it last summer he had tried to reach Mars. The trip, the story of which is told elsewhere, had not been entirely successful. But the ship had got back safely, and now Uncle Ben was getting it ready to take another cruise out into space.

Freddy, the pig, and his friend Jinx, the black cat, on their way up to the ship, were picking their path among the black stubs. Pretty soon they had to cross the brook. The water was high, so instead of just jumping over as they usually did, they went along to where they could get across on some stepping-stones that Uncle Ben had placed in the water, to be used when he had to carry pieces of equipment up to the ship. Jinx dashed across; then he turned and looked back. "Look out for that second stone, Freddy," he said. "It's prob'ly wobbly."

"Prob'ly wobbly, hey?" said Freddy. "That's a good one. Well, I'll be careful. I bet that water's rilly chilly."

"Swallow a lot of it and it'll cause ya nausea," Jinx replied, and then laughed so hard at his own joke that he slipped off the bank into the edge of the stream.

The cat had only got his feet wet, but he was so mad that Freddy thought he'd better not laugh very hard. He picked his way carefully across the prob'ly-wobbly stone and the two walked on together without saying anything more.

There was hammering going on inside the ship. An iron ladder led up to a door in the upper part of the rocket, and the two animals climbed up and looked in. Uncle Ben and his assistant, old Mrs. Peppercorn, were working at the instrument panel. Mrs. Peppercorn said:

"I'll clip these red wires together, so's't'
They can be hitched to this here post."

Jinx looked at Freddy and winked. Mrs. Peppercorn was about the most unlikely co-pilot you could imagine on a space ship. She was a little old lady who lived in Centerboro. She had rather forced Uncle Ben to take her as passenger on the first trip into outer space. But she had been such a good sport, and, once she had had the working of the ship explained to her, had shown so much mechanical skill, that Uncle Ben had agreed to take her in as partner. The only troublesome thing about her was the habit, which was certainly growing on her, of making up bad poetry, and even using it in her everyday conversation. Uncle Ben drove into Centerboro and got her every morning and took her home every night.

Uncle Ben nodded and said something which sounded like "Mpfh," which was really saying quite a lot for him, for he almost never spoke a sentence longer than two syllables. He wasn't much of a talker.

"Hi, Uncle Ben," said Freddy, "we've got something to show you." He had on an old coat of Mr. Bean's so that he would have pockets to carry things in. Animals that don't talk much can carry things in their mouths, but Freddy did a good deal of talking, which meant that every time he said anything he'd have to drop whatever he was carrying and then pick it up again. For talking with your mouth full is impolite, and besides, nobody can understand you. So now Freddy pulled a newspaper out of his pocket and handed it to Uncle Ben.

Mrs. Peppercorn read the item out loud over Uncle Ben's shoulder.

"Hi, Uncle Ben—we have got something to show you!"

MARTIANS CAPTURED
Crew of Flying Saucer Trapped
by Former Centerboro, N.Y. Man

LANKSBURG, VA. MAY 4. *Early this morning Mr. Herbert Garble of St. Petersburg, Fla., passing through Lanksburg on his way north, captured the only Martians believed ever to have visited the earth. Mr. Garble was driving north to visit his sister at whose palatial residence in Centerboro, N.Y., he formerly resided. Having driven all night, he had drawn up by the roadside on the outskirts of Lanksburg to rest, when a loud buzzing aroused him, and a large saucer-shaped object passed over his head and landed in a near-by field. Mr. Garble started to investigate, but his movements evidently alarmed the occupants of the saucer, which gave out a brilliant flash of light and made off at tremendous speed.*

*However, Mr. Garble pursued his investigations, and on arriving at the spot he found six small creatures who had evidently been left behind. They are described as about eight inches tall, dressed in red, with short legs, long noses, and luxuriant red whiskers. Mr. Garble captured the creatures, who stated that they were inhabitants of the planet Mars and—*Mrs. Peppercorn stopped. "Stated?" she exclaimed. "Can the critters speak English?"

"It tells about that farther down," said Freddy. "They claim they've been here many times, and have learned the language."

"Well, I suppose if they've come here once, they could have come before," said Mrs. Peppercorn.

"Mr. Boom," said Uncle Ben suddenly.

"Just what I was thinking," Freddy said. "Lanksburg is where Mr. Boomschmidt's circus has been spending the winter. That's what seems so funny about it. Here's Mr. Garble, who's from Centerboro and certainly no friend to us animals on Mr. Bean's farm, and here's Mr. Boom, who's a great friend of ours, and both of 'em in Lanksburg. And then—see what it says down here?—they've gone into partnership. Mr. Garble captured the Martians, and then he got to thinking that there'd be a lot of money in exhibiting them. So he remembered that Mr. Boom was wintering in Lanksburg, and he went to see him. And he's going to travel with the circus this summer and exhibit 'em."

"Money," said Uncle Ben.

"You bet," said Jinx. "Have a side show with real live Martians—I bet people'd pay fifty cents just to look at 'em."

"If your Mr. Boom is fool enough to join up with that good-for-nothing Garble he won't have much circus left by fall," said Mrs. Peppercorn. "Martians or no Martians. If he ties up with Garble," she added, "his fate will be har'ble."

"Ouch!" said Jinx.

Mrs. Peppercorn glared at him. "All right," she said, "let's hear you make a better rhyme."

"If with Garble he joins, he'll be full of aches and poins," said Jinx, and ducked down the ladder as she made a swipe at him with a screwdriver.

But Freddy was thoughtful. "We've had a lot of trouble with Mr. Garble one time and another," he said. "I wish Mr. Boom hadn't taken him into the circus."

Mrs. Peppercorn, who had been continuing to read the newspaper article, said: "We've got to see these Martians. Be a big help to find out what the folks on Mars are like before we get there, though I can tell you right now I don't approve of 'em."

Jinx said: "The paper says old Boom was so excited about having Martians in his show that he started right away getting ready for the road. How soon can we expect them in Centerboro, Freddy?"

"Depends on how many shows they give on the way north," Freddy said. "Usually Mr. Boom comes straight to Centerboro and opens his season with two or three days there, on account of having so many friends in the neighborhood. That takes about a week. But he'll probably think he ought to give at least one show in Washington, because I suppose the President will want to see them, and all the senators will want to ask them questions and find out if they are Republicans or Democrats—"

"It says here they wear red clothes," said Mrs. Peppercorn. "There ain't any doubt in my mind what they are."

"Why, they're Martians," said Jinx.

"Nonsense!" said the old lady. "Communists, that's what they are! They ought to be sent right back to Rooshia, where they came from! Garble oughtn't to introduce ya to anyone from Rooshia."

"Oh, now, wait a minute!" said Freddy. "What's Russia got to do with it? A Martian wouldn't even know that there was a Russia, much less a Communist."

"Then what do they wear red suits for?" she retorted. "And good land, don't they always call Mars the Red Planet?"

"That's because it looks sort of red in the sky," Freddy said. "My goodness, Santa Claus wears a red suit—you don't call him a Communist, do you?"

"I wouldn't put it past him," Mrs. Peppercorn said. "Seems like you can't trust anybody these days. And he lives right up there at the North Pole, handy to Rooshia."

"I shouldn't think you'd want to go to Mars," said Jinx, "if it's all inhabited by little Communists eight inches high, in red suits."

"I want to go more than ever now," said the old lady. "They ought to be investigated, hadn't they? Well, if there won't anybody else do it, I'll do it myself. And when I've investigated I'll have 'em arrestigated," she added.

Uncle Ben hadn't been paying much attention to an argument which he evidently thought rather silly. But now he folded up the paper and said: "Must see Martians. Who's going?" He looked around at them, and then started down the ladder to the ground.

The others looked at one another for a moment. "Where's he off to now?" said Mrs. Peppercorn.

"Golly, I guess to Lanksburg to look at the Martians," Freddy said. "Come on, he won't wait for us." And they scrambled down the ladder and hurried after Uncle Ben. They didn't catch up with him until they reached the barnyard where he was just climbing into his old station wagon. They piled in after him.

Mrs. Bean was sitting on the back porch in

her rocking chair. Now she leaned forward. "If you stop at the grocery, Uncle Ben, bring me back—here, I'll make you a list; you'll forget half of 'em if I don't." She started to get up, but Freddy ran across and explained quickly where they were going.

"Good grief!" she exclaimed. "Martians! Mr. B.!" she called. And as Mr. Bean came to the door: "Here's Uncle Ben going down to Virginia to see some folks from Mars. Don't you want to go along?"

But after a little talk, both Mr. and Mrs. Bean decided that they'd wait until the circus came to Centerboro to see the Martians. "You go along," Mr. Bean said. "Have a good time and don't forget to send us some postcards."

So they got into the station wagon and hung on tight to their seats. And Uncle Ben started the engine. It was an engine he had put in himself, the Benjamin Bean Atomic Engine—the small economy size, not the large battleship size —and it had so much power that when it started, with a whoosh and a roar, you had to have a good grip on the seats or you were likely to be left behind. It almost seemed to gather its wheels under it and jump, it started so fast. In three seconds it was out of the gate and streaking up the road.

Back on the porch Mrs. Bean smiled placidly. "I do like to see our animals having so much fun, Mr. B.," she said.

"By cracky," said Mr. Bean, "if ridin' with Uncle Ben's fun, I guess I'd as soon be sick abed. Why that start, it like to snapped old Mrs. Peppercorn's head right smack off her shoulders."

CHAPTER

2

Forty-eight hours after the capture of the Martians by Mr. Herbert Garble, Boomschmidt's Stupendous & Unexcelled Circus was on the road. Mr. Boomschmidt and Mademoiselle Rose, the bareback rider (who was Mrs. Boomschmidt in private life), came first, in a big red limousine with the Boomschmidt coat of arms in gold on the doors. Then came the red-and-gold wagons in which the dangerous wild animals lived. Only, instead of being in the cages, the lions and tigers were usually sitting up beside the driver, or even driving the horses themselves. For, as Mr. Boomschmidt explained when people expressed surprise at this arrangement: "Animals aren't really wild except when they're shut up. My goodness," he said, "you'd be wild yourself if you had to live in a cage."

And indeed his animals were always polite and well behaved, and in the towns where they had given shows summer after summer they had hosts of friends. On Sundays, when no shows were given, you could hardly ever find a single animal on the circus grounds—they would all be invited out to Sunday dinner by people in the town.

After the wild-animal wagons came the elephants and zebras and old Uncle Bill, the buffalo, and a lot of other animals, and then the little houses on wheels in which the circus people lived. There weren't as many of these as there had been in the early days, for more and more of the circus work was done by animals instead of humans. Elephants can put up a tent as quickly as men can, and almost any animal can be trained to sell tickets, or drive cars, or do clerical work. It had always been Mr. Boom's ambition to have an all-animal circus, and now all his performers in the main tent were animals except Mademoiselle Rose.

In the side shows, of course, there were some people. There was Madame Delphine, the gypsy fortune-teller, whose real name was Annie Carraway. She was Mlle. Rose's mother. And there was a new side show this year— the strong man. He was Mr. Boomschmidt's brother, Mr. Hercules Boomschmidt, and he looked exactly like Mr. Boomschmidt except that he was twice as tall and twice as wide. He looked like Mr. Boomschmidt seen through a large magnifying glass. He did a weight-lifting act, and sometimes in the big tent he sang in a quartet made up, besides himself, of the lion, a hippopotamus named Andrew, and Uncle Bill, the buffalo. It was really something to hear them render "Asleep in the Deep," or "Down by the Old Mill Stream." For they all had deep bass voices; Mr. Hercules, who was the tenor, sounded, even when he hit a high one, like the bass viol in the orchestra; and when Andrew really got down to work, it was like nothing but a thunderstorm coming up on the other side of the mountain.

And of course now there were the Martians.

There hadn't been time to give them much of a build-up, but Mr. Boomschmidt didn't think they needed it. He had some signs painted: "Men from Mars. They have come a million miles to visit you." And there were pictures of little red men climbing out of a flying saucer, with planets and comets zipping around. He had the carpenter build some little chairs and tables and other furniture, and fit up one of the wagons like a room that was supposed to be from a Martian house. And then the Martians were to sit around in the room and just talk and have their meals and do whatever they did at home on Mars, while the people filed past at fifty cents a head and stared at them. Mr. Garble would be standing by to answer questions.

It was plain before they started out that the show could stay right in Lanksburg all summer and make more money than it ever had before. For as soon as news that the Martians were with the circus came out in the newspapers, people from near-by towns came crowding into the city in the hope of catching sight of them. Mr. Garble wanted to stay right there. "Folks'll drive here from all over the country," he had said. "Instead of giving your regular show, we'll buy a couple hundred cots and put 'em up in the big tent and rent 'em out at five dollars a night. We'll turn the Martian side show into the main show and up the price to two dollars a night. There's seven dollars a head we'll make out of everybody that spends the night, and then there's all the people that'll just stop long enough to see the Martians and then drive on. I bet we can clear seven or eight thousand dollars a day."

Mr. Boomschmidt had replied that that was fine, only it wasn't going to be that way. "My goodness me," he said, "what do you suppose all those people up in New York and Pennsylvania and Connecticut and a dozen other states are going to say when they hear we're not coming this year? They're all my friends, and friends of my animals, and good gracious, you don't think I'd disappoint them, do you? And there's my animals—how do you think they'd like it to sit around and watch the crowd all going in to look at half a dozen stupid little peewees in red suits that can't even turn a somersault?"

"But think of the money," said Mr. Garble.

"You think of it," said Mr. Boomschmidt. "I'm thinking of my friends. We're going straight up to Centerboro and give our first show there."

But they didn't. For the newspapers in Washington, as well as everywhere else in the country, had the story about the Martians in

them, and the President happened to see a paper one day and he sent a high-up official in the
State Department down to request Mr. Boomschmidt to stop in Washington and give a special performance for the Cabinet and the Members of the Congress. So the circus went straight
up to Washington and put up the big tent and
gave a performance right in the White House
grounds.

Mr. Boomschmidt said they ought to give the
performance free. Mr. Garble didn't like that
much. He couldn't do anything about the main
show, but when the crowd began filing in to see
the Martians, he went and stood beside the
door with some tickets in his hand. He hoped
maybe the Congressmen would think they had
to pay even if he didn't ask them to. But they
just pushed right past him, pretending not to
see the tickets. The President was the only one
who paid. He insisted on buying tickets for his
wife and himself. He paid a dollar, and later
Mr. Boomschmidt bought that dollar bill from
Mr. Garble for a dollar and a half, and he had
it framed and hung up beside the speedometer
on the dashboard of his limousine. He was
pretty proud of that dollar bill.

Two days after leaving the farm, the station
wagon, with Uncle Ben and Mrs. Peppercorn

on the front seat, and Jinx and Freddy bounding around on the back seat, came roaring down into Washington and stopped in front of the White House with a jerk that all but sent the entire party through the windshield.

"If there's one thing I insist on in a car," said Freddy sarcastically, feeling of his nose, which had banged hard into the seat-back in front of him, "it's first-class brakes."

Mrs. Peppercorn, who had been straightening her bonnet, which had been knocked over one eye, stopped and sat up straight. "I hear music," she said.

Uncle Ben grinned. "Should think you might, ma'am," he said. "Brakes little tight, seemingly. Made your ears ring."

"By golly, it really is music!" said Jinx. "Yes sir—why, listen!" And he began to sing:

"Boom—be quick! Buy a ticket at the wicket!
Boom—get your pink lemonade. Get your
*   gum!"*
Boom—get your peanuts, popcorn, lollypops—"

And then Freddy and Mrs. Peppercorn joined in:

"Boom—Mr. Boom—Mr. Boomschmidt's
*   come!"*

It was the marching song of the circus, and as they watched, around the corner ahead of them came the big red limousine, and behind it, two by two, all the animals, with the elephants leading. On the back of old Hannibal rode the six Martians. They had little red handkerchiefs which they waved at the President, who waved back at them from the White House window; and all the Congressmen, who were grouped about the front porch, cheered and waved. There was some pushing and shoving to get in the front row, and one small Senator got knocked down and stepped on. He got mad and next day made a speech on the radio about it, saying that the President ought to have turned his back instead of saluting those Commies. "Waving their red flags right in front of the White House!" he shouted. "What is this country coming to?" But nobody paid any attention to him.

Uncle Ben started his engine, the station wagon gathered its wheels under it and bounded out into the middle of the street, spun around with a series of loud bangs, and ran jerkily alongside Mr. Boomschmidt's car. Everybody in the station wagon tried to yell *Hello*—except of course Uncle Ben, who just touched his hat to Mlle. Rose—and Mr. Boomschmidt and Mlle. Rose tried to yell back, but the street was

On the back of old Hannibal rode the six Martians.

jammed with people, all of whom were cheering madly and waving to the Martians, so nobody could hear anything.

It was like that all the way north. Even when they took the back country roads, people seemed to get word somehow that the famous Martians were in the vicinity, and they came running across the fields and scrambling over fences and driving their cars cross-country, until the road would be so thick with them that the elephants had to be sent ahead to clear a way for the wagons.

At night they camped by the roadside. Mr. Boomschmidt put several small tents at the disposal of the party from the Bean farm, and they had pleasant evenings about the campfire, singing songs and telling stories. Mr. Garble seldom took part. He and Freddy had fought more than once, and indeed Mr. Garble was never a person that anyone cared to be friendly with. For that reason it was impossible for either Freddy or Mrs. Peppercorn to talk to the Martians about conditions on their home planet. Mr. Garble wouldn't let them near the Martian wagon.

On the road Mr. Garble wanted to keep the Martians out of sight; he didn't think people ought to see them unless they paid. But Mr. Boomschmidt said that as long as the circus couldn't stop to give any shows he thought it would be mean to keep all these people from getting a look at them. At last, one evening by the campfire, when the exhausted Martians had gone to bed and most of the sightseers had left for home, Mr. Garble got really angry.

"You're making us lose money," he shouted. "These people are getting the Martians for nothing!"

"Oh, my gracious," said Mr. Boomschmidt, "*you* got them for nothing yourself, didn't you?"

"What's that got to do with it?" asked Mr. Garble.

"Do with it!" Mr. Boomschmidt exclaimed. "Oh, dear me, why I should think it had everything to do with it. Wouldn't you, Leo?" He appealed to the lion. "Why, here's Mr. Garble saying that it hasn't anything to do with it that he got the Martians for nothing."

"Hasn't anything to do with what?" the lion asked.

"That's just it," said Mr. Boomschmidt. "He doesn't say. Do with *what*, Mr. Garble? Oh, dear me, do please tell us, so we'll have some idea what we're talking about."

This of course was just Mr. Boomschmidt's usual way of winning an argument. He got his opponents so confused that they didn't know finally what they had been talking about. And in the end they were quite likely to agree to something that they had been fighting hard against five minutes earlier.

Now Mr. Garble made the mistake of trying to set Mr. Boomschmidt right. "The fact that I got the Martians for nothing," he said slowly, "has nothing—now wait a minute, I want to get this straight—has nothing to do with the fact that we're losing money by letting these people see the Martians free."

"Oh, dear, dear," said Mr. Boomschmidt. "Now really, I don't think you've got it straight at all. Do you, Leo? Because we aren't *losing* money, are we? You mean, if we shut the Martians up in their wagon, we'll have more money at the end of the day than if we let them ride where everybody can see 'em? My, my! If you can show me how we can do that, I'll say shut 'em up."

"Oh, that isn't it at *all*," said Mr. Garble. "I just mean—" And then he stopped. "I mean—" he began, and stopped again. Then he made a dreadful face, put up his hands and pulled out two large handfuls of hair, and turned and walked slowly away.

"Well, you shut *him* up anyway, chief," said Leo.

"For a little while, I guess," said Mr. Boomschmidt. "But Freddy's right: we're going to have more trouble with him. Maybe this Martian show was a mistake."

CHAPTER

3

The circus was nearly ten days getting up to Centerboro, and in all that time Freddy didn't find a single chance to talk to the Martians. Mr. Garble chased him away with a stick. But it wasn't so easy to chase Mrs. Peppercorn away.

"See here, young Herbert," she said to him, the first time he warned her away from the wagon in which the Martians were living, "don't you give me any of your sass. You stand aside and let me talk to these critters."

"I'm sorry, ma'am," said Mr. Garble, "but we can't have the Martians annoyed by idle curiosity. If there's anything you wish to know about them, you may address yourself to me."

"Oh, I may!" she said sarcastically. "When I had you in the fifth grade and addressed myself to you, I don't seem to remember that you ever knew the answers to anything."

Mr. Garble turned a little red, for a number of animals had come up to see what the argument was about, and Mrs. Peppercorn had indeed been his fifth-grade teacher, and knew a lot of things about him that were not entirely to his credit. But he stood his ground. "That was a long time ago," he said.

"Not so long that I've forgotten a lot of pretty silly things," she retorted. "Remember when you were reading something about 'the land of Egypt' and you called it 'the land of Egg-wiped'?"

"I did that a'purpose," said Mr. Garble sullenly. "I was trying to be funny."

"Land sakes, you never had to try! Remember that little Ella Tingley you were so sweet on?" She looked around at her audience, which now numbered nearly a dozen—among them

Hercules Boomschmidt. "This will amuse you, Mr. Hercules," she said. She always called him Mr. Hercules, though everyone else just called him Herc. "This here Herbie Garble, he gave Ella a five-cent bag of gum drops. But then I guess he got to wishin' he'd kept it himself—he wasn't ever much of a hand for being generous —and he sneaked back in during recess and reached in her desk where he'd seen her put it. But I guess Ella sort of figured what might happen, and she'd set a mouse-trap which it went snap! on Herbie's finger. Well, sir, he set up the most awful roaring and bawling you ever heard. Ella was watching behind the door and I guess she felt sorry for him, for she came in and put her arm around him, and he—well, Herbert, you remember, don't you?—you kicked her. And then—"

But Mr. Garble, who had been getting redder and redder, was now a deep purple, and he shouted suddenly: "Oh, shut up!" And then he turned and shoved through the ring of laughing animals, which was now two deep, and hurried off.

Mrs. Peppercorn smiled at her audience. "There's a lot of things Herbie don't like being reminded of. And I guess," she added, "there ain't anybody knows more about 'em than me.

Keep me from talking to his Martians! Just let him try!"

"You started to tell about after he kicked her," said Willy, the boa constrictor.

"That's the part he didn't want me to tell," she said. "Why, Ella, she had kind of a temper, and she picked up a bottle of mucilage and emptied it over his head. Of course his mother washed it out when he got home. But I don't know, he was kind of sticky all the rest of the year. The other children claimed that he stuck to things. Some said he stuck particularly to small things that didn't belong to him.

"There was another funny thing, too," she added. "They never got that mucilage smell out of him. After all these years, at night when the air gets damp, he still smells of it a little."

"Don't seem to me you ought to talk that way behind his back," said Andrew, the hippo, mildly.

"Oh, it don't?" she snapped. "Well, you bring him back here and I'll say it to his face. I've done that often enough, just the same as all the other teachers he ever had. Miss Plaskett, she had him in the seventh grade, she used to make him turn out his pockets every half hour. She said you'd be surprised what you'd find. She said she wished she had him for a piggy bank—she could quit teaching."

Mr. Hercules suddenly began making strange sounds. "Huh!" he said in his deep voice. "'Huh—huh!" Although he looked so much like Mr. Boomschmidt, he wasn't really like him at all. His mind was as slow and heavy as his brother's was quick, and he had only one expression on his face where Mr. Boom had a hundred. Now his face didn't change at all, but the animals knew he was laughing. "Huh, huh!" he grunted. "Caught in a mouse-trap! Uh, uh!" He had just begun to laugh about the mouse-trap; in an hour or so he would get to the mucilage and begin to laugh about that. He wasn't very quick to get a joke but when he did get it, it stayed got. He would be rumbling with laughter about this for a week.

Now with Mr. Garble out of the way there was nothing to prevent Mrs. Peppercorn from interviewing the Martians. She went over to the wagon which had been fitted up as a house for them. Of course it was only a wild-animal cage with bars on the sides, but there were six little beds at one end, with red coverlets, and on six pegs over them hung six small red nightshirts. In the middle was a doll's dinner table, Martian size, which was about four inches high, with a red checked tablecloth and dishes and silver and everything. At the other end was their living room, with six little overstuffed chairs, and a table on which was a vase with forget-me-nots in it. There were a lot of other things scattered about; on the wall there were even pictures of the solar system and of the planets and the moon and so on. At one end was a little door, so that the Martians could get in and out. It wouldn't have been safe for them to walk around the grounds when the crowds were there, but sometimes late at night two or three of them might be seen strolling about, arm in arm.

One of the Martians got up from his chair and came over towards Mrs. Peppercorn. He walked oddly, she thought, like a dog walking on its hind legs. He was dressed all in red, he even had red gloves on his tiny hands and red cloth shoes on his long feet, and his black beady eyes stared at her expressionlessly over a fluff of red whiskers that hid all but the tip of his extremely long nose. He bowed to her, rubbing his hands together—and looking, she thought, very much like Mr. Metacarpus, the floorwalker in the Busy Bee in Centerboro.

"Yes, madam?" he said politely.

"You speaka da Eenglish?" Mrs. Peppercorn demanded in a loud voice. Since she was speaking to a foreigner, Mrs. Peppercorn, like many other people, thought that in order to be under-

"You speaka da Eenglish?" Mrs. Peppercorn demanded.

stood she would have to shout, and because his English was probably bad, she thought he would understand if she spoke bad English too. Nobody knows why people do this in addressing a foreigner, but it is a fact that they always do. Some people even talk baby talk to them.

"Yes, madam," replied the Martian. "I speak English. And I am indeed happy to welcome you to our little home from home, our little corner of Mars in your wonderful America." His voice was oily, and he bowed in a humble way when he had finished.

"Land sakes!" said Mrs. Peppercorn. "Why you do speak English real good. Understand you learned it here?"

"We have made many trips to your beautiful country, yes."

"Well, I tried hard enough to get to yours last summer. But our space ship pilot, he got sort of mixed up and landed us back on earth."

"Ah, yes," said the Martian. "I have heard of this. You are, I believe, Mrs. Cornpopper?"

"Peppercorn, Peppercorn!" said the old lady sharply. "And how might you be called?"

"It is a little hard to pronounce for an earth dweller," he said. "In Martian, it is spelled S-i-m-g-h-k."

"Goodness!" said Mrs. Peppercorn.

"The *i* is silent," he added helpfully.

"The whole thing can stay silent for all of me," she replied. "Well, Mr. Martian, what's it like on Mars? We're planning to try again to get there, and we'd sort of like to know what we'll find. Folks be pleasant to us, you think?"

"Perhaps they would ask you to join a circus," he said.

Mrs. Peppercorn frowned and stared at him suspiciously. "You get funny with me, young man," she said, "and you'll get your ears boxed."

"Oh, ma'am!" he said. "How can you imagine I would attempt to poke fun at so talented a lady? No, no, madam; I and my fellow Martians consider ourselves most fortunate in having been asked to join a circus. We wish to travel and see your country, to observe your manners and customs—and what better way could we have found?"

"Well, I expect maybe that's so," said Mrs. Peppercorn. "If you don't mind being stared at, and probably poked and prodded, by a lot a zanies who're never so happy as when they're peekin' through somebody else's keyhole."

"Curiosity towards other worlds is only natural," said the Martian. "It was curiosity that brought us here, just as it was curiosity that made you try to reach Mars last summer. I'm told you took a pig with you. That seemed to us, back on Mars—excuse me, tee-hee"—he tittered behind his hand— "that seemed funny. Hardly an animal that *we* would choose for company on a long trip—"

"Now just stop right there," said Mrs. Peppercorn. "Nobody's going to miscall that pig when I'm around. He's the most famous pig in the country, and he's my friend, and I'm proud of it. You mean to say that up on Mars you've never heard of Freddy?"

"Freddy?" The Martian shook his head. "Freddy," he said thoughtfully. "No . . . no, can't say I have. Though, wait!" He slapped his forehead with his hand. "Yes, we have heard of an obscure detective of that name. Up in York State, wasn't it? Tried to set himself up in the poetry business, didn't he? Of course! How we laughed! The poetic pig! Oh, dear, ma'am," he said suddenly, "I'm afraid I've offended you. Do not be angry, I beg. We are so ignorant of your earthly ways. I'm sure he must be a wonderful poet."

"Well, well, don't overdo it," said Mrs. Peppercorn impatiently. "He's a good poet, I don't deny. Good, sound rhymes, maybe a little ordi-nary by the highest standards. I expect he just tries to do too much. He flies his own plane, he runs the First Animal Bank, and as a detective —well, there ain't anybody can touch him in the whole country. I give him that. But you can't do that and be a poet, too. No, sir, my idea of poetry is something that everybody ain't done before. You don't use the old rhymes, like 'love' and 'dove' and 'eyes' and 'sighs.' You make words rhyme that nobody has ever rhymed before. Like, say, in 'The Night Before Christmas.' It goes like this:

" *''Twas the night before Christmas, and all*
    through the house
Not a creature was stirring, not even a mouse.'

"Well, sir, that's the kind of rhymes Freddy uses. But the way I'd write it, it goes like this:

" *'All through the house 'twas the night before*
    Christmas.
     Not a creature
     Would meet yer,
      Neither Mr. nor Miss Mouse.' "

"Phooey!" said the Martian. The five other Martians, who had been dozing in their chairs, sat up with a jerk. "You can't make such horrible verses in *this* house," one of them muttered angrily.

But Mrs. Peppercorn went right on. "Now, what have you got?" she said. "Instead of one ordinary rhyme: 'house' and 'mouse,' you've got two brand new ones: 'creature' and 'meet yer,' and 'Christmas' and 'Miss Mouse.'

"Now let me recite for you my poem about the universe. It isn't very long, only about seven thousand verses, and every one of 'em as bright and clear as a new penny.

> *"Some stars are large, some stars are small,*
> *And some are quite invisiball . . ."*

Two hours later when the dinner bell rang over in the big dining tent, all six Martians were asleep in their overstuffed chairs, and Mrs. Peppercorn was on line 5,226 of her long poem. And she hadn't found out a single thing about what life was like on Mars.

CHAPTER

4

Mr. Boomschmidt was so happy about all the money the circus had taken in in Washington that Freddy put off warning him against Mr. Garble. And after all, what was there to say? Millions of people would pay fifty cents to see real live Martians. They'd drive hundreds of

miles just to get a look at the creatures. The
half-dollars would drop into the cash box as
fast as you could keep the line of people moving, and the show could stay in one place for
months. To warn Mr. Boomschmidt against
Mr. Garble would be to warn him against making a lot of money. Mr. Boom would just
laugh.

"Just the same," Freddy said one day to Leo,
"I don't like it. Every time I've had anything
to do with Garble it has meant trouble."

"Trouble for Garble, you mean," said the
lion. "Old Garble knows when he's well off; he
won't start anything. Not as long as the dough
keeps rolling in."

"I know," Freddy said. "But I don't trust
him. I can't help feeling that there's something
wrong about this Martian business. I wish they
hadn't gone into partnership."

"Oh, for Pete's sake!" said Leo irritably.
"The chief has never made much money with
his circus. Now he's got a chance to make a lot
this summer, and you want to bust it up, just
because you don't like Garble. Let the poor old
chap alone, can't you?"

"Well, don't cry over it," said Freddy. "Mr.
Boom has always made a good living. And you
know he cares a lot less about making money
than he does about having his animals be happy

and have a good time. Oh, all right, I won't say anything to him. But as long as Garble is around here, look out for trouble, that's all."

But no trouble came, for a while anyway. Mrs. Peppercorn tried three times to get some information from the Martians about what their planet was like, but each time the conversation got somehow onto poetry, and the interview ended with the old lady reciting and the Martians asleep. So Uncle Ben decided to go home and get on with the work on the space ship.

"Coming?" he asked Freddy.

But Freddy said he and Jinx would stay with the circus. "I think I know how we can get an interview with the Martians," he said. "You go ahead. We'll be along in about a week, and maybe we'll have some information for you."

"Atmosphere," said Uncle Ben.

"Yes, I'll try to find out about the air on Mars," Freddy said. "But it must be O.K. for us: these people breathe our air all right."

So Freddy and Jinx and Mrs. Peppercorn stayed with the circus as it rolled on north. But they had no luck getting information from the Martians, who had evidently been warned not to talk to them. Mr. Garble no longer bothered to chase them away, for the Martians just turned their backs when either the pig or the cat came up to the wagon, and refused to say a word.

Mr. Boomschmidt was in a hurry to get to Centerboro, so the circus stayed on the road until dark, then made a quick camp, and started on in the morning as early as he could get his animals up. Most of them got right up when they were called, for they had many friends in Centerboro and were anxious to get there. It was usually Andrew who held things up. The hippo was a hard sleeper, and he was so big and had such a thick skin that it wasn't easy to wake him. You could slap him and poke him with sticks, and even shoot off guns and bang on his head with a shovel, but he'd just go right on snoring. Mr. Boomschmidt found that the easiest way to rouse him was to jump up and down on his stomach. After a few minutes he'd come to and want his breakfast. The jumping up and down made him feel hungry: "Gives me kind of a gnawing sensation," he said.

It was just about dark one evening when Freddy, in a trench coat and a felt hat which he had borrowed from Bill Wonks, came up to the Martian cage. Mr. Garble had gone to the dining tent to get his supper, and the Martians, who had had theirs, were in their little red

The easiest way to rouse him was to jump up and down
on his stomach.

nightshirts and just about to go to bed. Freddy noticed that they still had their red gloves on, and even their cloth shoes.

He said: "Good evening, gentlemen. I represent the United States Immigration Bureau. I am informed that you entered this country without a permit, and that you have no passports. You realize that this is a serious offense, and that you can be deported and sent back to your own country. However, the Government has no wish to cause you unnecessary trouble. Perhaps the matter can be arranged. Would you mind answering a few questions?"

The Martians went into a huddle for a minute, and then the one who spelled his name Simghk came over towards the front of the cage. It was the first time Freddy had had a close look at any of them, but he had waited until dusk to visit them because he didn't want them to see through his disguise, so he really couldn't see much.

The Martian said: "Our manager, Mr. Garble, would be the person to see. But of course we are quite willing to answer your questions. We have nothing to hide."

In his experience as a detective, Freddy had found that those who were always protesting that they had nothing to hide were usually concealing some pretty awful stuff. But all he wanted to know now was what conditions would be like on Mars. So he said: "I'll ask my questions of Mr. Garble, then. But as long as I am here, maybe you wouldn't mind telling me one or two things—I mean, these are my own questions, nothing to do with immigration. I'm just curious to know what it is like to live on your beautiful planet."

Simghk said it was a good deal like living on earth: they lived in the same kind of houses—only smaller, of course—and ate the same kind of food, and breathed the same air.

Freddy asked one or two more questions, and then he began to feel that there was something queer about the Martian's answers. Life on Mars wasn't exactly the same as life on earth—it couldn't be. The books he had read had told him that the air on Mars was much thinner than on earth, that a man who weighed 150 pounds here would weigh only about 60 pounds there, that the Martian year was nearly seven hundred days long. Those were only a few of the differences. Yet everything Simghk said might have been said about life on earth. So now Freddy said: "Your climate must be a lot hotter than ours, since Mars is so much nearer the sun than the earth is."

"Yes," said the Martian, "but not as much hotter as you might think. Delightfully cool evenings, even on the hottest days."

Freddy was satisfied now; he knew everything he needed to know. But, more out of curiosity than anything else, he asked one final question. "Of course you don't call your planet 'Mars,' in your Martian language. Would you tell me what you do call it?"

"Gladly, my dear fellow, gladly," said Simghk. "Our name for it is—perhaps I'd better spell it: S-m-b-l-y-f."

"Ah, indeed," said Freddy. "And I suppose the *y* is silent? You wouldn't be kidding me, would you?"

"No more than you're kidding me," was the reply. "You know, we have a word in Martian for you. It's spelled P-l-i-k-g and the *l* and *k* are silent. It's pronounced *oink-oink*. Expressive, isn't it? I doubt, though, if your Mrs. Peppercorn would be able to find a rhyme for it."

So the Martian knew who he was, Freddy thought. Well, what of it? "Oh, I don't know," he said. "Though why should she want to?

> *"There isn't any poink
> In finding rhymes for* oink."

The Martian shuddered. "Skip it," he said hastily. "Skip it. More than ten thousand verses of that kind of stuff we've listened to! Mister, we're flesh and blood, just like you. We can't take much more of it."

Freddy grinned at him. "I'll go tell her you want to hear that universe poem over again." And he nodded and walked hastily away, followed by the pleading voice of the Martian, begging him not to summon Mrs. Peppercorn.

But of course he didn't summon her. As soon as supper was over, he got Mrs. Peppercorn and Jinx one side. "Those fellows aren't Martians," he said. "Everything he told me proves that they haven't the faintest idea what things are like on Mars. For instance, I said that Mars must be hotter, since it is nearer the sun than we are; and he said yes, it was. But Mars is farther from the sun, and therefore a lot colder. He said the air was like ours. But it isn't; we couldn't breathe in it. Oh, there were a dozen things. I said there were four moons, and he agreed. But there are only two. I tell you, these Martians are fakes."

"I ain't a bit surprised," said Mrs. Peppercorn. "Mostly, anything Herbie Garble touches is something different from what he says it is. But if they ain't Martians what are they?"

Freddy shook his head, and Jinx said: "You know, there's something kind of familiar about 'em, at that. But I can't put a claw on it." He grinned. "Wish I could get a claw on one of them for a few minutes. I'd soon find out."

"Well, we can't tell Mr. Boom," Freddy said. "If he knew they were fakes he wouldn't keep 'em in the show a minute. And my goodness, everybody in the country—yes, and all over the world—has heard about them, and hopes to see them. You know what would happen if the Martians left the circus. Half the people would laugh their heads off at Mr. Boom for being fooled, and the other half would be mad at him for getting them all excited about Mars. And none of them would ever go to his show again. Golly, I think the only thing we can do now is pretend we think they're the real thing, and play along for a break. Maybe when we get back home, somebody will think of something."

They left it at that.

CHAPTER

5

ENTER H

The day the circus gave its first show in Centerboro, every road leading into town was jammed
for miles with sightseers. They came in cars
and wagons, on foot, on horseback, and on bi-
cyles; several hundred flew in by plane. The
big attraction of course was the Martian cage.
It had a side-show tent to itself, at the door of

which Mr. Garble stood and took the money. He had a barrel beside him, and when it was full of fifty-cent pieces and bills, he nailed the head on and rolled it over into a corner and brought out another empty barrel. By the end of the evening performance he had six full barrels, ready to be taken over to the bank.

Some people filed through two or three times, and each time paid fifty cents apiece. The hardest job was to keep the line of people moving. Mr. Garble had hired three men who stood behind it and said: "Move along, please, step lively, others are waiting." And if anybody stopped to stare for even five seconds, one of the men would push him along.

The main show did pretty well, too. For after people had satisfied their curiosity about the Martians there wasn't anything else for them to do but look in at the big tent. Mr. Boomschmidt was pretty happy, because he got all the money that the big tent took in, as well as ten cents out of every fifty from the Martian tent.

But Mr. Garble wasn't happy. If Mr. Garble had been making a million dollars a minute, he still would have been unhappy because he wasn't making a million and a half. He was that kind of man. So he tried all sorts of schemes. He tried to move the people through the tent faster. One day he shoved the line through at a trot, but the people couldn't see anything and they made such a fuss that he had to let them go through again free. He wanted to raise the admission to a dollar, but he had advertised it at fifty cents, and he couldn't get away with that either. So then he said Mr. Boomschmidt was getting too much money out of the Martians, and wanted him to take only five, instead of ten cents out of every half-dollar.

Maybe if he had been nice about it, Mr. Boomschmidt would have agreed. But he stormed and roared and said that he was being cheated, and a lot of things like that. So Mr. Boomschmidt said: "Why, my gracious, Mr. Garble, I didn't know you felt like that about me. What a terrible person I am, to be sure! My, my, Leo," he said, turning to the lion, "ain't I awful!"

"You sure are, chief," said Leo, who had an idea where an argument was going.

"Yes, sir," said Mr. Boomschmidt, "it makes me kind of sick to think about myself, I'm so mean. Don't suppose there's a bit of hope for me either, is there, Leo?"

"No there ain't, chief. Not a smidgen."

"Dear, dear—you hear him, Mr. Garble? Guess you'll never get anywhere with an old skinflint like me. My goodness, you called me that yourself, and I wouldn't want to make a liar out of you. Folks have got to live up to the opinion that other folks have of 'em. Can't go changing your character at my time of life. So I guess I better take fifteen cents out of every half-dollar, instead of ten. Eh, Leo?" He pushed his silk hat to the back of his head and smiled happily. "Well, well, I'm glad that's settled. Now Mr. Garble, if we—"

Mr. Garble interrupted with a roar. "Hey! You can't *do* that! I want you to take five instead of ten, which it's only fair you should do so. Nobody said anything about fifteen!"

"Why, I did—didn't I, Leo? Good gracious, I'm only trying to live up to your opinion of me. That's what my mother always wanted me to do. 'Orestes,' she'd say, 'I want you always to live up to my opinion of you.' But, dear me, if you're going to be offended, we'll just say no more about it. Let's just leave it at ten cents, eh?"

"Ten!" Mr. Garble shouted. "I said five."

"So you did, so you did," Mr. Boomschmidt replied. "And I said fifteen. So we split the difference, and agree on ten. That's the best way to come to an agreement. Each side gives way a little. Then everybody's satisfied."

"But ten cents is just what you were getting before!" howled Mr. Garble, almost beside himself with rage and confusion.

"Well, upon my word! So it is!" Mr. Boomschmidt was astonished. "Well, Leo, what do you know about that! Everybody satisfied and we don't have to change anything. Now isn't that nice!"

Mr. Garble jumped up and down, he was so mad. He didn't say anything more. As he turned and stamped away, he grabbed the hair over his ears with both hands and tugged. A lot of it came out.

"He'll be bald as a squash before you get through with him, chief," said the lion.

"Goodness, Leo, do you think so? Oh, I do hope not; he's not very pretty now, I don't believe we'd like him around—though maybe we could exhibit him. Poor Mr. Garble, he's bald as a marble. Dear, dear, I do hope I've not got this poetry thing from Mrs. Peppercorn. Do you suppose it's catching?"

"Look, chief," said Leo, "let's be serious for a minute. Do you know what a lot of your animals are saying?—yes, and lots of the Centerboro folks, too—they're saying that while Garble and his Martians were just a side show when he started out with you, now *we're* the side show, and he's the main show. What they're afraid is that he'll take the circus right away from you."

"Pooh!" said Mr. Boomschmidt. "Now you're being silly."

"Yeah?" said Leo. "Suppose he takes his Martians and sets up a show on the other side of town. How much business will our show do?"

"Why, I guess about as much as it always did. Some folks in these towns come year after year, Martians or no Martians. I'd miss those dimes I get from Garble's admissions, but my gracious, we've always got along before. I guess we'd keep on."

The lion said: "Maybe. But I was down getting my mane waved and set yesterday—"

"Oh dear, oh dear," Mr. Boomschmidt interrupted. "Have you been going to beauty shops again? Really, Leo— Well now, your mane does look nice; but do they have to pour all that perfumery over you?"

"Oh, lay off, chief," said Leo, looking embarrassed. "That isn't perfumery; it's some stuff they put on to make the hair curl better."

"Good gracious!" said Mr. Boomschmidt. "They don't have to soak you in it! It made my hair curl just smelling it, and if—"

"Look," the lion interrupted firmly, "if you're just going to be funny, I'll go get some of the others so they can enjoy the comedy too. But if you want to hear what I've got to say—"

So Mr. Boomschmidt apologized and said sure he did, and what was it?

"Well," said Leo, "you know what places those beauty shops are for gossip—"

"My, my, don't I just!" Mr. Boomschmidt exclaimed. "I just dropped in yesterday to have my eyelashes curled, and—" He came to a stop at sight of the reproachful look on the lion's face. "Oh, dear," he said, "I've hurt your feelings again. Go on, Leo; go on."

"Well, if you're quite through," said the lion severely. "What I'm trying to tell you is the kind of thing people were saying. This operator that sets my mane, she said to me: 'When's your new boss going to take over the circus?' I said: 'New boss? What are you talking about?' and she said she'd heard Mrs. Underdunk—that's old Garble's sister, you know—she'd heard her telling some other woman that her brother was buying you out. And a couple of other women were talking about how they'd heard how Garble was going to get him some animals and start a circus in competition with you. Then he'd have a circus *with* Martians, and you'd have one *without* Martians, and who do you think would make the most money?"

"Pooh," said Mr. Boomschmidt. "What do I

care how much money Garble makes? All the good you can get out of money is the fun you have spending it, and Garble never spends any of his, so who has the most fun?"

"Yeah?" said Leo. "Well, I'll tell you how he's spending some of his; he's hired a talent scout—you know, like the movie companies have, to go round and find animals who can dance or sing or do special tricks. He's got a hen already that can whistle Dixie. Keeps her up at his sister's house. When he gets enough animals, he'll start his own circus.

Mr. Boomschmidt said "Pooh!" again. After all, it had taken him a good many years to get his circus together; it would be a good many more before Mr. Garble was able to give him any competition. And a hen that could whistle "Dixie" wasn't going to make much of a circus, even with Martians on the side. "Besides," he said, "Garble has got to stay with me for a year. I've got an agreement in writing. I bet his hen will get sick of whistling "Dixie" to him before that year is up. Just the same," he said, "maybe we ought to do something. Two circuses in the same town. My, that would be bad."

"That's what I'm telling you, chief. It'll be awful bad."

"Well, I know that, Leo," Mr. Boom- schmidt said irritably. "Of course I know that.

Don't just keep repeating everything I say and trying to look wise as if you'd got a brand new idea. Think!"

But it isn't easy to think with somebody standing right over you to see that you do it. The lion scowled fiercely and stared down at the ground so hard that he was almost cross-eyed. He glanced up once or twice to find that Mr. Boomschmidt was still standing there watching him. Then he concentrated harder than ever. The next time he looked up, Mr. Boomschmidt was gone.

CHAPTER

6

Two days later Mr. Hercules Boomschmidt began to laugh about the mucilage being poured
over Mr. Garble's head. Every time he saw Mr.
Garble he would stop and begin to heave with
laughter. "Mucilage!" he would say. "Uh, uh,
uh!" Of course the other animals saw him, and
they picked it up. They would imitate Mr.

Hercules's heavy pronunciation of the word. "Moosiludge! Uh, uh!" Mr. Garble got pretty sick of it.

At last he complained to Mr. Boomschmidt. "There isn't anything I can do about it," Mr. Boom said. "Herc will get over it, and then the others will quit bothering you. He always gets over a joke in a week or two."

"A week or two!" Mr. Garble shouted.

"Hardly ever takes longer than that," said Mr. Boomschmidt. "Of course, if you can think up another good joke, something funny to tell him that might take the place of the—the mucilage, and get him to laughing about that . . . You see, Herc can never handle more than one joke at a time."

So Mr. Garble went downtown and bought a joke book, and then when he saw Mr. Hercules, and before the other could begin to laugh, he'd say quickly: "Hi, Herc: say, have you heard this one?" And he'd tell him a joke. Mr. Hercules would listen attentively, and when Mr. Garble finished and made a great show of guffawing and slapping his knee, he'd say "Yuh." And then he'd begin to heave. "Moosiludge!" he'd say. "Uh, uh!" Mr. Garble didn't get anywhere.

The Bean farm was only a few miles from Centerboro, and after the first day, Freddy and

Jinx drove back home with Uncle Ben. The Martians were a problem that the pig was worried about, but he had work to do—his newspaper, the *Bean Home News,* to get out, and the affairs of the First Animal Bank to attend to. And there was an unfinished poem, which went like this:

> *"I think that I shall never see*
> *Another pig as smart as me;*
>
> *A pig so full of zip and zest,*
> *A pig so fashionably dressed,*
>
> *A pig so gay, a pig so free,*
> *A pig so quick at repartee.*
>
> *Who bears with fortitude the pain*
> *Of knowing that he's rather plain.*
>
> *Although not handsome, you'll admit*
> *He rather has the best of it:*
>
> *Some genius might invent a yak,*
> *An alligator or macaque,*
>
> *Or other animals, small or big—*
> *But no one could invent a pig!"*

The poem wasn't really unfinished, of course. But Freddy thought that a few changes should be made. As it stood, he was afraid that it might sound a little conceited.

And with all this work on hand, he wasn't doing any good hanging around the circus grounds. Besides, every day the Boomschmidts, or one or two of the circus animals, would come out to visit their friends at the farm. Often he, or others of the farm animals, would go into town and spend the night with circus friends.

Mr. and Mrs. Bean hitched up Hank, the old white horse, to the buggy and drove down to see the show and have a look at the Martians. Uncle Ben could have driven them down, of course, in a matter of minutes, but they said no, they preferred the buggy. Uncle Ben said they ought to get used to modern travel, but Mrs. Bean said that since modern travel evidently meant getting the living daylights jounced out of you, she guessed they'd stick to the old-fashioned way.

One night after the circus had been in Centerboro a week, Freddy had been entertaining Willy, the boa constrictor. They had spent a happy evening in the cow barn with Mrs. Wiggins, the cow, and her two sisters, Mrs. Wurzburger and Mrs. Wogus, and some of the other animals, telling stories and singing and playing games, and it was nearly midnight when Freddy and Willy finally went back to the pig pen to sleep. Freddy politely offered Willy his bed, but the snake said no, he'd be much more comfortable just coiled up in the armchair. Freddy continued to insist and Willy to decline, and there was a great exchange of politenesses, and it was nearly one before they finally settled down, Willy in the chair and Freddy in the bed. And at two there was an agitated clucking outside the window, and then a series of hard, woodpeckerlike taps on the door.

Boa constrictors are heavy sleepers, especially when they have just eaten, and Willy, while not really full, had had a couple of pans of johnnycake and a dozen large jelly sandwiches—part of the refreshments which Mrs. Bean had kindly provided for the evening. Freddy, too, was never one to leave the table until the last crumb had vanished, and perhaps he had been a little overanxious to prove that a pig could hold as much as any snake—anyway he had eaten more than he usually did. Neither of the sleepers stirred.

The tapping was redoubled; then, as there was no answer, it stopped for a minute or two. The duet of the two fellow snorers had not missed a single note. But then came the one sound which will wake any farm animal, no matter how deeply he may be dreaming—the crow of a rooster, just outside the door.

Freddy came to in an instant and jumped up. "What—what is it?" he gasped, then went to the chair and shook Willy. "Hey, time to get up!" he shouted. But then he became aware that it was still dark outside. He went to the door and threw it open. Charles, the rooster, and his wife, Henrietta, were on the threshold.

"Hey, what's the *matter* with you, Charles?" Freddy demanded angrily. "Making all this rumpus, and it hasn't even begun to get light yet! You clear out, before I—" Here he stopped abruptly, and turned back into the pig pen, for Henrietta had darted past him and flown at the boa. She was flapping and fluttering and pecking at his head with her strong beak, and all the time screeching: "Murderer! Chicken thief! What have you done with my daughter Chiquita? And her brother, Little Broiler? Answer me, you great squirming low-down good-for-nothing beast! Answer me before I tear you to pieces!"

Willy, still half asleep, blinked and ducked as he uncoiled his fifteen-foot length from the armchair. He could have knocked Henrietta flat with one slap of his tail, but he was good tempered, even for a boa. "Hey, hey!" he hissed protestingly. "Lay off, sister. What's the matter ails you?" And then, as a particularly sharp peck landed on the end of his nose: "Oh, *quit!*" he said crossly, and suddenly whipped a coil of his body around the hen and held her fast.

"Lay off, sister."

Charles was still on the doorstep, and Freddy, now thoroughly awake, turned to him. "'What's got into you two?" he demanded crossly. "Coming around here and crowing in the middle of the night, and attacking my guest—"

But Charles, in his turn, brushed past Freddy and went up to the boa. "Sir," he said haughtily, "that hen is my wife. Release her immediately or it will be the worse for you."

"I'll release her if she'll quit trying to poke my eyes out," said Willy, and Freddy said: "Let her go." He took a broom from behind the door. "Henrietta, if you don't shut up this minute, I'm going to let you have this right across the cackler."

To his surprise, Henrietta did not reply. The reason was that, before releasing her, Willy, who, like all boas, always hugged a little harder than he meant to, had given her an extra squeeze, and there wasn't any breath left in her.

"Well, Charles," Freddy said, "perhaps you'd like to give some explanation of why you've come roaring around here in the middle of the night and disturbing me and my guest when we're peacefully sleeping."

"You may have been sleeping," said Charles, "but it sure wasn't peaceful—not with the racket you were making. And let me tell you, sir," he went on, "if you will select as guest such a low, scoundrelly sneak, such a base miscreant, as this ravaging roost-robber—why then, sir, you deserve a far more dire punishment than merely to be roused from your sodden slumbers by the clear buglelike tones of my powerful voice. You ask me why I crowed. It was the only way to wake you. For we have come here to ask—nay, to demand—either the restitution of our son and daughter to their rightful perch in the home from which they were so savagely and cruelly snatched scarcely an hour ago, or the immediate execution of this villain, this low circus actor, whose very appearance brands him as guilty. As for you—"

"Just a minute," Freddy interrupted. "Guilty of what? As far as I can make out, you object that we were snoring. Well, go on away home and you won't hear us. Anyway, we don't either of us snore, do we, Willy?"

"Certainly don't," said the boa. "Freddy, can't you get rid of these people? I'd like to go back to sleep. Yes, and I'll snore if I want to, too, and how do you like that, rooster?" He darted his head at Charles and his pointed tongue flickered in and out so rapidly that the rooster felt a little dizzy, watching it. He backed off.

"Have a care, sir," he said. "Let me tell you,

I am not to be trifled with. Beware how you arouse my wrath, for within this feathered bosom, sir, beats the heart of a lion, the—"

"Oh, shut up," said Freddy, "or you'll get a wallop on your feathered bosom with this broomstick. Now clear out, both of you."

Menaced with the broom, Charles withdrew into the night, still making courageous noises. But Henrietta, who had recovered her breath, said: "I'm not leaving here until you do something about this, Freddy. Now you listen to me. You know the revolving door that Mr. Bean had put in the hen house last year—well, a little while ago it squeaked and woke me up. Little Broiler had been sleeping on the perch beside me, and he wasn't there. I looked all around, and then I discovered Chiquita was missing, too.

"Freddy, it's a long time since anything like this has happened. Not since Simon and his family of rats lived under the barn. But you went and invited this snake to visit you; I must say, I thought you had better sense. Of all the criminally stupid things to do—"

"Oh, now, wait a minute!" Willy put in. "I didn't eat your squawking brats—I beg your pardon, your sweet little feathered angels— since that's what you seem to be accusing me of. Good heavens, after all I had at the party, do you think I'd want a mouthful of bones and feathers for dessert?"

"Bones and feathers indeed!" Charles exclaimed. "I'll thank you to keep a civil tongue in your head. If you think you can come here and insult my family—"

"Oh, shut up, Charles," Freddy said. "He didn't come here to insult 'em or to eat 'em. He came here as my guest to have a good time. Will you tell me how, even if he'd wanted to, he could have got into the hen house and eaten Chiquita and Broiler?"

"How!" Henrietta exclaimed. "Why, you know that revolving door. There's no way of locking it. You push it and it just goes round and then you're inside. All he had to do was to —was to—" She stopped short.

"Yeah," said Freddy. "All he had to do was get in. And if you can tell me how a fifteen-foot snake can get in through a revolving door—"

"Oh, my goodness!" said Henrietta, and put one claw up to cover her face. "Oh! Oh, I could die of shame!" Then she put her claw down and resolutely faced Willy. "Sir, how can you ever forgive me! To accuse you of such murderous conduct! But I was so worried—" She broke off, then gave a loud squawk. "But what am I saying! I *am* worried! Chiquita! Little

Broiler! Then where are they? Charles, *do* something!"

"Yes, my dear; yes." Charles stepped forward, the picture of quiet efficiency. "Just leave it to me." He bowed to Willy. "We ask your pardon, sir, for our suspicions. Groundless suspicions, as we should have realized. But we were naturally somewhat upset—"

"*Somewhat* upset!" Henrietta cackled. "*Somewhat!* When some monster has kidnapped and probably devoured two of our children! You ninnyhammer! You numbskull! You fine-feathered windbag! Go out there and find them!"

Charles had no desire to go stumbling about in the night in search of some chicken-eating monster. Anyway, how was he to find his children if they had already been devoured? He hesitated, shifting from one foot to the other. But Willy came to the rescue. "Well," he said resignedly, "I'm broad awake now—don't suppose I'll get asleep again very easily. I'll go with you, Charles. I don't believe there's any monster around. We'll probably find that those two have just stepped out to get a little air."

At another time Henrietta would have taken this remark as reflecting on her housekeeping, by suggesting that the hen house was a little stuffy—as, of course, with Charles and Henrietta and thirty-five children in it, it certainly was. But now she only said: "That's very kind of you." Then she turned to Freddy. "Will you come over to the hen house? Maybe there'll be some clues."

So Freddy got his flashlight and his magnifying glass, and he put on his Sherlock Holmes cap with the peak in front and the one in back; and then after a moment's thought he hooked his false beard over his ears. "Because," he said vaguely, "you never know what you may run into." Really, of course, he was just playing The Great Detective to an imaginary audience.

Not that there's any harm in that. A lot of his best detective work had been done when he was pretending in this way.

CHAPTER

7

It was plain that since the revolving door of the hen house was only large enough to let chickens go in and out, the kidnapper must have been a small animal.

"Might be a weasel," Freddy said. "We cleaned all the rats out of this neighborhood several years ago." He turned on his flashlight and began to examine the door, and at once all the thirty-three remaining chickens began a great fluttering and squawking. So Henrietta went inside to quiet them.

Freddy went on with his examination. He turned the door slowly, and with flashlight and magnifying glass went over every inch of the four leaves. Then he looked around on the ground. He got as far inside the door as he could, which wasn't very far, because only his head would go in. "H'm," he said. "Ha!" And then he gave a screech that could have been heard for half a mile.

Charles and Willy were standing back, watching the great detective do his stuff. Willy's expression was awestruck—or would have been, if a snake can express such an emotion. It was really just snakelike. Not that he knew what Freddy was doing. But it astonished him that Freddy should do anything.

Charles, too, watched attentively, but with a patronizing air, nodding now and then to himself as if saying: "Ah, yes, that's very well done; that's just as I would have done it." Though the rooster of course knew no more than the snake what Freddy was up to. He couldn't very well, because as a matter of fact Freddy didn't know himself. He was just doing his Big Detective act.

When Freddy screeched, Willy said excitedly: "Golly, he must have found something."

"Possibly a clue," said the rooster. "Very capable fellow, Freddy—very. One of my—" Then he stopped. He had intended to say: "One of my most promising pupils," but then he remembered that Willy had known Freddy long enough not to be taken in by such a boast.

Freddy, however, had not found a clue. If you stick your head in a revolving door, and don't go all the way in, and then if somebody tries to come out from the other side, and pushes, your head will be caught and you won't be able to get it out until they stop pushing. This was what had happened. Henrietta had started out, and when Freddy got caught and yelled, she pushed harder than ever, so as to get out and see what was going on. The louder he yelled the harder she pushed, and if Willy hadn't grabbed the flashlight and turned it on the pig, so she could see through the glass how she was squeezing his neck between the edge of the door and the jamb, she might have injured him seriously.

When he got loose, Freddy had to lie down to get his breath. Henrietta stood beside him and fanned him with a wing, and she said: "I'm very sorry, Freddy. But why didn't you call to me?"

"Call!" he exclaimed. "You can't call when you're being choked to death."

"Nonsense!" said the hen. "You couldn't have been choked much, the way you were bellowing. Anybody's being choked can't even squeak."

"Bellowing!" said Freddy indignantly. "How could I bellow when . . . Why, look at my neck!"

There were indeed marks on each side of Freddy's neck, but when Henrietta brushed them with her wing, they disappeared. "Just dust from the edge of the door," she said. "I guess you were more frightened than hurt, Freddy."

"All right! All right!" Freddy got up. "If that's the thanks I get—"

The general disturbance and Freddy's yells had waked up some of the other farm animals, and now Jinx and Mrs. Wiggins and the two dogs, Robert and Georgie, came over to the hen house to see what was going on.

Since there was no sign of the robber, nor of the vanished chickens, Freddy asked the dogs to sniff around and see if they could get the scent of any stranger. If they could, it might be possible to track down the kidnapper and re-store the chickens to the bosom of their family. That is, if they hadn't been eaten up.

Since there were no feathers around, it was certain that they hadn't been eaten on the spot, and it seemed likely then that the thief intended to take them to some quiet place where feathers wouldn't be noticed. So Robert and Georgie sniffed around hopefully. Finally Georgie announced that he thought he'd picked up a strange scent, and he called the others to see if they could detect anything.

Jinx said he thought there was a slight smell of marshmallows. Freddy said the predominant smell was old dusty carpets, though there was a faint undertone of boiled cabbage. Willy couldn't smell anything.

"Well, I don't believe any kidnapper ever smelled of marshmallows and carpets and cabbage," Mrs. Wiggins said. "Let me smell." She gave a couple of strong sniffs, but she blew her breath out instead of drawing it in and raised so much dust that it set them all sneezing.

"When you're all through snorting," Henri-etta said acidly, "how about doing something about my children?"

"That's right," Freddy said. "We're wast-ing valuable time. Georgie, how about that strange scent you thought you picked up?"

The little brown dog said: "It's right here, if you want it. 'Tisn't marshmallow or cabbage; for my money it's rat."

"Rat!" said Freddy incredulously, and Jinx said: "Pooh, there hasn't been a sign of a rat around here in a year."

"O.K.," said Georgie. "Have it your way."

"Georgie's right," said Robert, the big collie. "Hadn't we better trail him? Because he may not yet have—" He stopped, with a glance at Henrietta.

"May not have eaten them—that's what you mean," said the hen flatly. "Well, let's say it right out and then get going, not stand here talking all night."

So the two dogs started on—sniff, sniff, sniff —up along the edge of the barnyard, and through the pasture toward the woods, and the others followed.

If the robber was a rat, Freddy didn't have much hope of getting the two chickens back. Rats sometimes steal young chickens, but they seldom carry them far. There were several puzzling things about the affair. How had a rat managed to carry off two chickens? And why had he selected, as one of them, Little Broiler, who, although his mother's favorite, was a scrawny little creature? Why, with thirty-five to choose among, hadn't he picked out a plumper specimen for his late supper?

The trail led across the brook below the duck pond, and then up into the woods. Here Mrs. Wiggins turned back. "You folks go on," she said. "Last time I was up in these woods I sprained a horn, catching it on a branch, and that was daylight. I'll go round up some of the rabbits and see if they've seen anything. It'll be daylight in another hour."

Freddy didn't like dark woods much either. It wasn't that he was a coward. Faced with a real danger, he could be as brave as anyone. Or almost. But he had a vivid imagination, and to such people imaginary dangers are much more awful than real ones. He knew that if he went into the woods he would begin trying to scare himself, he would imagine gnarled, taloned fingers reaching out to clutch him from behind every bush, and hideous false faces peering around tree trunks. The very thought of what he would try to make himself see made his tail come uncurled.

Yet the Great Detective must not falter. So when the dogs went sniff-sniff up into the deeper gloom among the trees, with Jinx and Willy beside them, ready to pounce, and with Charles, poked along by Henrietta, following after, he gave a sigh and went on.

At any moment a great dry claw might fall upon his shoulder.

"It's rat all right," said Robert in an under-tone. "Scent's easier to get on these damp leaves."

These woods of Mr. Bean's were fairly open; even though he could see very little in the blackness, Freddy managed to follow without stumbling. His imagination, however, was getting in some good licks. There was a gorilla with horns grinning horribly at him from that dark clump of bushes that he could just make out close to his right hand. And that faint, regular sound—heavy, soft footsteps padding remorselessly along behind him! At any moment a great dry claw might fall upon his shoulder, and pull him back— A twig, released by someone ahead, whipped back and slashed him across the nose, and he gave a sharp squeal of terror.

The others stopped. "Hey, we ought to be quiet," said Robert reprovingly. "What's wrong?"

"Nothing—er—nothing," Freddy stammered. "I just—well, it was just something that—that came back to me suddenly." It certainly had come back suddenly, he thought. And then he heard the regular sound again and realized that it was his heart.

"We're coming out on the back road," said Georgie. "That's why it seems lighter now."

They came out close to a little bridge that

carried the road over the brook, and Charles said: "Ha, how well I remember this historic spot." He struck an attitude. "You recall, no doubt, my friends, how on a certain day I here met and defeated a full-sized rat in fair and open combat. On that day I struck a blow for freedom that was heard around the civilized globe. The name of Charles—famous already in legend and story—"

"Psst! Pipe down," Freddy whispered. "Something up the road there. Looks like a car. Move up along the ditch and let's see."

It was a car, all right. As they crept closer, a starter whined, the engine started, then, without putting on its lights, the car gathered speed as it moved off towards town.

The dogs began sniffing around where the car had stood, but Henrietta said sarcastically: "I thought we were looking for rats. What do we care about the car? The rat didn't drive away in it."

"No," said Robert, "but he was right up here by it. That's funny—he was all around it. There's a queer smell here, too. Not rat. Something different."

"Funny, I smell it, too," Freddy said. "It's familiar, somehow. Now, where—"

"Hey!" Georgie called. He was up by the stone wall. "Your rat's gone in here, I think."

And he began to dig furiously at the foot of the wall where there was an old woodchuck hole.

The others moved up, but scattered when the stones and earth from Georgie's digging flew about their ears. "Take it easy!" Freddy said. "You can't dig him out; you'll have this old wall down on top of you before you get a big enough hole to get at him."

"That's right," said Robert. He sniffed at the hole. "He's there all right, but we'll just have to sit and wait till he comes out. That's your job, Jinx."

"Let me try," said Willy. He put his head down the hole a little way, then drew it out. "Well, I'll try it. I'd like a bigger hole though, if you've got one in stock. Look, if I get stuck you'll have to pull me out. I'll thump my tail twice—then you pull." He went down the hole again. Five feet of him disappeared, then he stopped.

For a long minute nothing happened. The ten feet of Willy that had not gone down the woodchuck hole moved a little, then was still, then wriggled more violently. And then the tail thumped twice. "He's stuck!" said Freddy. "Catch hold, everybody."

They all rushed forward—then stopped and stared at one another. On a snake, of course, there isn't anything to catch hold of.

"For Pete's sake," said Jinx, "what are we going to do? I can't pull on anything unless I get my claws into it. Could you get a hold on his tail with your jaws without biting him, Freddy?"

"I don't see how," said the pig. "But if we can't take hold of him, he'll have to grab hold of us. I wish he could hear us. But maybe this will work." He went over and pulled a rail off the fence on the other side of the road, and dragged it across Willy. The snake seemed to understand, for he immediately whipped a double coil around it. "All right," said Freddy, "now catch hold of the rail. No, get on this side and push." And all pushing, they dragged Willy out, like a cork out of a bottle. Then they left the rail and ran up to the front end of the snake to see what had happened. He couldn't tell them, for he had a large, mean looking rat in his mouth.

"Well, upon my soul," said Freddy, "if it isn't our old friend Simon!"

CHAPTER

8

Simon was the head of a large family of rats which had given the Bean animals a great deal of trouble in the past. Time and again they had been driven away from the farm, only to return when they were least expected. The old Grimby house, up in the Big Woods near where Uncle Ben was working on his space ship, had been their headquarters for a time. That house had burned down last year. But the cellar was still there, and part of the floor hadn't burned. When Willy pulled Simon out of the woodchuck hole, Freddy wondered if the rats had moved back into their old home.

The boa put his captive down in the road. He said: "I guess this guy just ducked down that hole when he heard us coming. Nobody's been living in it for a long time. It's just a dead end and there's no sign of chickens."

It was beginning to get light now. Simon knew he had no chance to escape; before he could take two jumps either Jinx or Willy would pounce and drag him back. He snarled at them and started to say something, but before he could begin Henrietta was on him, tearing at him with beak and claws and beating him with her wings. "Where are my children?" she screamed. "You tell me what you've done with them, or I'll—"

"This isn't getting us anywhere," Freddy said, "and she'll only get hurt." For the rat was defending himself by slashing at her with his long yellow teeth. The pig nodded to Willy, who quickly threw a loop about the hen and held her tight.

When the boa had squeezed her a little to make her keep quiet, Freddy said: "Well, Simon, last time I saw you, you promised Mrs. Bean that you wouldn't ever come back to this farm—remember? How about it?"

"Well, well," said Simon, pretending to recognize the pig for the first time, "if it isn't Freddy the Snoop! Peeked through any good keyholes lately, Freddy? Aren't you kind of off your beat? This road doesn't belong to old Bean. I've as good a right here as anybody."

"Sure," said Freddy. "But you didn't have a right down by our hen house tonight. You didn't have a right to kidnap two of Henrietta's children."

"Dear me," said the rat, "are two of them missing? Kidnapped, I think you said? That grieves me deeply." He giggled maliciously. "It'll grieve the kidnapper more, if he tries to eat them, for a scrawnier lot I never saw."

"Look, rat," said Jinx, "Henrietta heard the revolving door squeak. She looked and found two chickens missing. She sent for us, and Robert and Georgie trailed you up here. We've got you dead to rights."

"The silly part of your story is about trailing me," said Simon. "Those two couldn't trail a regiment of skunks across a field, even if they were only two feet behind. I haven't been near your old hen house. If I want to exercise my jaws I can find an old boot somewhere to chew

"Well, well, if it isn't Freddy the Snoop."

on; I don't have to ruin my digestion on a lot of rubber bands with feathers on 'em."

"O.K.," said Jinx, "you asked for it." He knew that Simon, like most rats, was ticklish, and now he pounced on him and tickled him unmercifully. Simon wriggled and screeched, and all the time Jinx talked to him: "How *do* you make those noises, Simon? . . . Boy, you sure get some queer sound effects . . . I like to hear 'em . . . Of course I'll stop—any time you're willing to tell the truth, eh? . . . That's pretty; let's do that one again."

At last the rat couldn't take any more, and he gasped that he'd talk if only Jinx would quit.

He had indeed, he said, been down by the hen house. But he hadn't been inside. He had been passing by, and it had been just an impulse that had led him to stop in and look over a place where he had spent so many happy hours in the past.

"You never spent any happy hours in our hen house," said Charles.

"The farm, you stupid cock-a-doodle, the farm!" Simon snapped. "It was my home, in better times," he said, becoming sentimental again. "My family was born and raised there, in peace and contentment; no doubt we would still be living there if it were not for the envy and spitefulness of this cat here. And the silly ambition of this dumb pig to be a great detective. Had to detect something, so he discovered rats in the stable! About as clever a feat as discovering cows in the cow barn! And then he must drive us out, although the good Mr. Bean never grudged us the little grain we ate."

"Yeah?" said Freddy. "I suppose that's why he nailed tin over the rat holes."

"How little you understand him!" said Simon. "It was a game between us. All done in a spirit of good sportsmanship."

"Sure," Freddy said. "We're all good sports together. Well, you were just passing by. Where had you come from? Where were you going? And what have you done with those two chickens?"

"You've no right to ask me any questions at all—" Simon snarled.

"O.K., Jinx," put in Freddy.

"But," the rat added hastily, "I've nothing to hide. I came from Centerboro, where I went to have a look at those Martians, in the circus. And I was going back to where I have been living the last two years, and it's none of your business where that is; it's nowhere near the Bean farm. As for those chickens, I know nothing about them."

They questioned him some more, but that was all they could get out of him. Though he did admit that he had investigated the mysterious car that had driven off towards Centerboro when they had appeared on the road. "There was a man in it," Simon said, "and I thought he was asleep. If you want to know where the chickens are, you'd better find out what he'd been up to. I heard something moving ahead of me when I came up through the woods. Probably he stole your little darlings."

Jinx wanted to tickle him some more, but Freddy said no, and they took him down to the barn and padlocked him into an old parrot cage. There was really no proof against him, nothing to connect him with the theft of the chickens except the fact that he had been in the barnyard. He hadn't eaten them. If he'd stolen them, where were they?

Freddy wanted to go back to bed. But before he did he stopped in the cow barn to see Mrs. Wiggins. She had nothing to report. The rabbits she had interviewed had seen nothing, and only two had heard some squawking up in the pasture. Yes, it might have been chickens. But any bird, waked up suddenly, might make a noise like that.

Freddy was pretty discouraged. "Seems as if we ought to have done something," he said.

"Henrietta's in a terrible state. She wants to have Simon executed or something. But we really haven't got anything on him."

"She'll never get any information out of him if she has him executed, that's one thing sure," said the cow. "Not that you'd get anything out of him except lies, anyway. I'll go down and have a talk with her. Maybe I can calm her down. And you go get some sleep."

"I couldn't sleep a wink," Freddy said. "Not with all this on my mind."

Mrs. Wiggins was considerate, even for a cow. She didn't even smile. "Well, you try, anyway," she said.

So Freddy went up to the pig pen. Since he couldn't sleep, he didn't go to bed, but sat in his comfortable big chair. And three minutes later his head had fallen back and his eyes were shut and his mouth was open and he was breathing slowly and I'm afraid rather noisily. He certainly must have been pretty tired to act like that when he was wide awake.

Seven hours later, at noon, he was still so wide awake that Jinx, having knocked twice, came in and had to shake him hard before he opened his eyes.

"Wake up, my dear old Sherlock," said the cat. "Awake! Arise! To arms, my snoopy old sluggard! Your lordship's carriage awaits."

Freddy said: "Umph! Ah! Evenin', Jinx. Jus' doin' a little thinkin'."

"Well, snap out of it," Jinx said. "The time for thought has passed, the time for action has come. So open your eyes and shut your mouth and quit snoring. Mr. Boom has sent his car for you. He wants you right away."

"Wants *me?*" Freddy said. "What for?"

"Ask Herc. He's driving. But if you can get anything out of that dumb man-mountain you're smart, even for a pig."

"I'd better go," Freddy said. "But if you get time, Jinx, I wish you'd go up to the Big Woods and scout around. I've got a hunch you might fall over a rat or two."

Jinx said he would, and Freddy went out and got into the long, glittering car with the Boomschmidt arms on the door panels. He would have ridden in front, beside Mr. Hercules, but the latter said no, he must sit in back. In the fields they passed were cows and horses, on the walls and in the trees were chipmunks and squirrels and birds; all of them knew him, and waved; and Freddy waved back, graciously and with deep and lordly bows. He was having a lot of fun, pretending to be a king receiving the acclaim of the populace, until, as they got nearer town, they began to overtake people who were going in to the circus. These were mostly strangers, and although they had certainly heard of Freddy, they didn't recognize him, and many of them laughed, and two little boys thumbed their noses at him.

"Good gracious," Freddy said to himself, "I'd like to think that my crown isn't on straight, but that wasn't meant for the king, it was meant for me!" He glared at the little boys. "Wretched little brats!" The rest of the way he looked straight ahead with a very severe expression on his face. To his disgust, people laughed more than ever. I don't suppose you can blame them, for it was rather unusual to see a pig riding in the back seat of a luxurious limousine.

Now amid all this laughter Mr. Hercules had said nothing, but just before they got to the circus grounds, Freddy saw the strong man's shoulders shaking, and heard the familiar "Uh! Uh!" that meant he was laughing, too. This was too much. "Look, Herc," the pig said, "either you quit this silly laughing or else pull up and let me out. I'll walk the rest of the way."

Mr. Hercules shook his head. "Can't hulp ut," he said. "Every time uh think o' moosiludge uh have tuh laugh!" And he shook some more.

"Oh," said Freddy, "if that's all it is!

I thought . . . But it's time you were getting over that joke, isn't it?"

"Nope," said the other, " 's funny. Uh, uh!"

The main show was just starting in the big tent, and a line several hundred yards long was waiting to file through the Martian side show. Freddy found Mr. Boomschmidt sitting at his desk in the trailer where he and Mademoiselle Rose lived, pasting newspaper clippings in a scrapbook. He had his hat on the back of his head and he looked worried.

"Go see Garble, Freddy," he said. "He claims a gang of rats attacked his Martians last night and carried off one of 'em. Anyhow, one of 'em's missing. He says he's going to leave the show because he claims I haven't provided protection for his Martians. Well, we'd lose a lot of money, but 'tisn't that so much as—my goodness! can't you hear what people would say?"

"Sure, they'll say 'Good riddance to bad rubbish.' "

"Oh, no, Freddy; my gracious, no! Garble'll claim my circus is overrun with rats. He'll write to the newspapers, saying they're attacking the performers, and pretty soon they'll be attacking the customers. He'll warn people against coming to my show. No, my boy, we've got to get that Martian back. Or at least round up those rats."

"Garble won't work with me," Freddy said.

"He'll have to. It won't look very good if he refuses the help of the best detective in the state. Dear me, I can write to the newspapers too, can't I?"

They were silent for a minute, and from outside came the heavy voice of Mr. Hercules: "Moosiludge! Uh, uh!" Freddy glanced sharply at the little bottle with a brush in it which Mr. Boomschmidt had been using. He bent and sniffed of it. "So that's mucilage, eh?" he said. After a second's thought he brushed a lot of it on a blank sheet of paper which he folded several times. "I've got an idea," he said. "Would you have Herc drive right back to the farm and give this to Robert and ask him what it reminds him of?"

CHAPTER

9

Freddy had got to thinking what it would be like if he ever got to Mars. He wondered if he'd be homesick, and just in case he was, he composed a homesick song. He was humming it now as he went to look for Leo.

Way down upon the old home planet,
  Million miles away;
I'm so homesick I can hardly stan' it;
  There's where the old pigs stay.

Oh, my heart is weak as Jello
  Everywhere I fly;
Oh golly, how I sob and bellow,
  Far from the old home sty.

He found the lion over by the big tent, and asked him if he had heard about the rats.

Leo said: "Yeah. Gang of 'em pitched into those Martians when they were out taking a walk last night and kidnapped the head man. Or so they say."

"What do you mean?" Freddy asked.

"Why, nobody heard any fighting. Unless the Martians were taking the heck of a long walk. But they claim it was right by their wagon. Of course, they've got in the habit of wandering around a lot at night, and—"

"Hey, excuse me," said Freddy, jumping up. "Hi, Robert," he said, as the collie came trotting over to them. "What's the verdict?"

"I had Herc bring me back," Robert said. "Thought since the message was about mucilage, he might get it mixed up with his joke. Well, that's the same smell there was around that car. I guess you spotted it, didn't you—the smell of mucilage? And if Garble smells of mucilage when it's damp—like at night . . ."

"Yes. That was Garble up there on the back road, with his lights out, all right. Garble and Simon—they're in something together. My guess is, Garble was back of this kidnapping of Chiquita and Little Broiler. But how does that tie up with the Martian kidnapping?"

It was at this moment that Mr. Garble came up. "You—Freddy—whatever you call yourself," he said. "I have something I want you to give Mr. Benjamin Bean." He took a paper from his pocket and held it out. "I want him to get it today." He turned to the lion. "Leo," he said, "you can tell Mr. Boomschmidt that I'm taking my Martians and pulling out of here tonight." Then he walked quickly away.

Freddy glanced at the paper. He said: "Oh golly!"

"What's the matter?" Leo asked.

"I think it's a summons or something. To come into court and show cause why he should not within three days remove the ship or rocket from the premises known as the Big Woods, now the property of Mr. Herbert Garble.

"Oh golly," said Freddy again. "Garble must have bought the Big Woods and the Grimby house. Mr. Margarine owned that property. Oh golly, what will Uncle Ben do? He can't move the ship inside of a month."

He thought for a minute. Then he said: "The thing is perfectly plain, and why I didn't see it before I can't imagine. Garble was up on the back road last night. So was Simon. I've no doubt that they had something to do with the kidnapping of the two chickens. That hooks up Garble with the rats. But Garble is also hooked up with the Martians. Martians that we don't think are Martians. Martians, Leo, that *I* think are—"

"Rats!" Leo exclaimed. "Well, tint my eyebrows! Of course. They're the right size, and all covered up in those red clothes . . . And that head guy that is missing—the one they claim was kidnapped by rats—is Simon. They had to make up some story when he didn't get back. My gracious, Freddy, we ought to have tumbled to that long ago."

"We sure ought. But it's as well that we didn't. Because we'd have told Mr. Boom, and it's better if he doesn't know."

"Better!" Leo exclaimed. "I don't get it. Now that we know—why, come on, let's go down there and take Garble and his rats apart. Boy, will I shuck 'em out of those little red suits—"

But Freddy interrupted. "No, *no,* Leo! Anything like that is just out! We can't tell Mr. Boom—we can't tell anybody! Not anybody! Because if people find out that the circus has been putting on a fake Martian show—"

"I get it," said the lion. "Yeah, it would ruin the chief's reputation, wouldn't it? But Freddy, we have to do something!"

Freddy got up. "We're going to see Garble," he said. "We'll tell him Simon has confessed. Come on."

Just inside the entrance to the Martian tent, Mr. Garble was taking in the half-dollars. He was on his third barrel of the day. He wore a broad smile, as he always did when money was passing through his hands into his pocket— which of course was what the barrel really was. Every now and then he would put an arm into the barrel and move his hand among the crackling, jingling contents, smiling more broadly, as if it were some particularly delicious soup he was stirring.

It wasn't a work that he liked to be interrupted in, and he scowled and shook his head at Freddy when the pig beckoned to him. So Freddy pushed in past the crowd in the doorway. "Sorry to trouble you, Mr. Garble," he said politely, "but I thought you'd want to know. We caught a rat last night up in the Big Woods. Funny thing about him is, he claims he

knows you. Says you hired him to play the part
of a Martian in your show. Says all the other
Martians are rats, too. Queer story, isn't it? I
bet after all this nationwide hullabaloo there's
been over the Martians, some newspaper would
be pretty glad to print it, don't you?"

Mr. Garble turned pale, and for a moment
he glared speechlessly at the pig. Then he
pulled himself together. "Pooh," he said, "nobody'd believe a ridiculous story like that!"

"No? Maybe Mr. Boom would," Freddy
said. "Maybe he'd pull the red suits off a couple
of your Martians. Maybe he'd find rats, eh?
What do you think he'd do?"

But Mr. Garble had now recovered enough
to smile nastily. "Maybe he'd kick you off the
circus grounds, pig—had that idea occurred
to you?" he asked.

"Look, Mr. Garble," Freddy said patiently,
"we've got the rat. We can prove that your Martians are fakes. But we'll make a deal with you.
We'll promise to say nothing about that. In return you'll quit talking about pulling out and
starting your own show. And you will promise
to allow Uncle Ben's space ship to stay in the
Big Woods until he is ready to start for Mars."

Well, Mr. Garble put up a lot of argument,
and he hollered and stamped and pulled out
some more hair, which wasn't easy to do when

he was trying to count money, and he was so upset that he let six people go into the tent free. But he knew that he was licked. Once it got out that the Martians were nothing but rats dressed up, not another half-dollar would tinkle into the barrel.

At last he said: "The Big Woods belong to me now, of course; I bought it from Mr. Margarine. But I haven't any wish to inconvenience Mr. Benjamin Bean, and I am willing to allow him to keep his ship there another month. However, I am not doing it because I take any stock in your ridiculous story. These Martians are Martians, that I can prove. But I admit that if you spread the story that they are rats, you could do my show some temporary harm. Therefore I am forced to agree to your terms."

"No you aren't," Freddy said. "If I told that story, and you could prove that it wasn't so, you could put me in jail and you'd make more money than ever."

"I don't want any trouble," said Mr. Garble. "No, ma'am," he said to a woman who wore a pink hat with poinsettias on it. "Children under fifteen are *not* free." Then to Freddy: "Now you get out of here, and take that big lummox with you."

"But I thought you didn't want to tell the

chief that they're rats," said Leo as they walked away.

"I don't," Freddy said. "I can't. But Garble doesn't know that. So that's one thing settled; he won't dare try to make Uncle Ben move the ship. But it doesn't settle our main problem; how we're going to get rid of those rats without making a monkey out of Mr. Boom. And it doesn't find Chiquita and Little Broiler for Henrietta."

"Seems to me we're stuck," said Leo. "We can't get rid of the rats, and yet we can't let 'em stay. Whatever we do is wrong."

Freddy said: "No. What's wrong is not to do anything. When everything seems like a hopeless mess, the thing to do is stir it up good. Then something always comes to the top that you can use. I'm going to give it a stir. Want to come back to the farm with me?"

Mr. Hercules drove them back to the farm. Jinx came into the barnyard as they drove up. "Just been up to the Grimby house," he said. "You were right about the rats. Must be a dozen or more of Simon's family living there. And boy, are they fresh! They claim the house belongs to them—say they've got a paper to prove it. I didn't argue with them—there's more than I could tackle alone. But now Leo is here, what do you say we go up and have a look at their paper?"

So they went, up across the pasture and into the woods, across the brook on the prob'ly-wobbly stone, past the rocket ship, from which came the sounds of hammering, and to the charred ruins of the Grimby house, where the terrible Ignormus had once had his headquarters. The chimney was still standing amid a tangle of blackened beams and partly burned boards, and against it leaned a sign which said: NO TRESPASSING. This Means You! H. Garble, Owner.

They looked at the sign for a moment, then Jinx shouted: "Hey, rats! Come out here. We want to talk to you."

But nobody answered. When he had called three times without result, he said: "Well, let's go down cellar. That's where they're living, I think." And he went towards the cellar door, whose wooden flaps had been laid back to reveal a flight of stone steps going down into darkness.

The three animals paused at the head of the steps. "Well, lead the way, lead the way, Jinx," Freddy said. "You know where they are."

"It's dark down there," Leo said. "What's the use going down if we can't see 'em when we get there?"

They looked at the sign.

"Are you sure that floor is safe?" Freddy asked. "We don't want it coming down on us when we're in there."

"Look, are you coming or aren't you?" Jinx demanded. "I'm not going down alone; there are too many of them."

"Sure we're coming," said Leo. "We aren't afraid of rats. But—well, how about goblins? My Uncle Ajax said you always wanted to look out for goblins in damp cellars."

"Pooh!" said Jinx. "There's no such thing as goblins, outside of fairy tales. Your Uncle Ajax was an old sissy."

"Oh, yeah?" replied the lion angrily. "My Uncle Ajax was a tough old fighter. But he said to me, he said: 'There's only two things, Leo, a lion ought to run from: one is spring house-cleaning, and the other is goblins.' "

"You ever seen a goblin?" Freddy asked.

"No, but my Uncle Ajax said they were little round-faced things, with big mouths and spindly legs, and they wore red-tasseled caps, and they sneak up behind in the dark and pinch you. He said if you ain't ever been pinched by goblins you ain't ever been really scared."

Freddy had walked away for a few steps and was looking up at the sky as if trying to decide if they might expect rain. Leo had sat down and appeared to be quite ready to go on reminiscing about his Uncle Ajax for another hour. Even Jinx had backed away a little from the cellar steps and had gathered his hind legs under him as if prepared to leap into flight in a red-tasseled cap was poked around the edge of the dark doorway. Of course none of them believed in goblins. But you don't have to believe in a thing to be scared of it.

Freddy was probably more scared than the other two. But he knew, too, more about why he was scared. He was scared because he was imagining how scary it would be to go down into that dark cellar and see, out of the corner of your eye, three or four little round, spindly-legged figures scampering out of sight. And he knew that the only way to get over being scared was to go right down there and search that cellar for goblins, until you were certain—or at least, until your imagination was certain—that there were no goblins there.

So he went to the edge of the steps, and then he hesitated, and then he went down halfway and called: "Hey, goblins, watch yourselves! We're coming in!"

And then what really scared him, as well as his two friends, so that they were right on the edge of turning and making a beeline for home, was a voice that came out of the cellar. "Come along, pig," it called in a sort of harsh pipe.

"Come right down into our parlor. Don't be scared. Nobody here but us goblins." And then there was laughter, peals of laughter from a dozen little goblin throats—or what sounded like goblin throats to Leo. Of course he knew the goblins couldn't be real, because he had made them up in the first place. But maybe that is what scared him most. He began backing slowly away.

But Freddy had recognized one voice among the laughters. "Hey, Ez," he called. "I hear you. Come on out. I want to talk to you." He went back up the steps, and a second or two later a rat came hopping up out of the cellar and sat up with his forepaws clasped in front of him. He bowed. "I believe—yes, it is Gentleman Freddy, the educated pig. And slinker Jinx. And—well, darn my union suit, if it isn't old frizzle-mane from the circus! Well, well, gentleman, to what happy circumstance do we owe the honor of this call?"

CHAPTER

10

The rat was Ezra, one of Simon's sons, and the interview with him was not very successful. It became almost immediately an exchange of more or less polite insults. Ezra said that he hoped that that stingy old Mr. Bean was well. "I wouldn't suppose, knowing what I do about him," the rat said to Freddy, "that he'd ever give you enough to eat, but I can see that you're still managing to—if I may use the expression —make a pig of yourself. You sure do bulge everywhere; I bet there isn't a lean strip of bacon on you."

Freddy said: "Thank you, you're very kind. Mr. Bean is quite well. And I trust that that frowzy old thief, your father, is in good health? And all his disgusting children? Including, of course, your estimable self? I'm most happy to hear it. Because it will be easier for you, when you're driven out of this house, to stay alive until you can find a new home—a long way from here."

"You're very good to say so," Ezra replied. "But of course we don't plan to leave here. We think it much more likely that the Beans—and of course you and the other animals—will find it—shall we say, pleasanter?—to look for a new home yourselves. After we have lived here for a while." He grinned wickedly. "You see my father has bought the Big Woods. He owns it. Mr. Garble bought it from Mr. Margarine, and my father bought it from Mr. Garble."

Freddy didn't believe a word of it. "How unfortunate for your father," he said. "I hope he didn't pay a big price for the woods. Because when he's kicked out Mr. Garble will certainly never give him back the money."

At last Ezra lost his temper. "Oh, shut up!" he snarled. "And get out of here! Can't you see that sign? You're trespassing and we can have you arrested for it."

"Not if we don't do any damage, you can't," Freddy replied. "That's what the law says."

"Shucks," said Leo, "let's *do* a little damage and see what they do about it." His big paw shot out like lightning and pinned the rat to the stone. "Don't wiggle or I'll have to put my weight on you, and boy, if I do they'll have to scrape you off this step with a pancake turner."

Ezra squealed angrily.

"You'll be sorry for this!" he said. "If you think you can walk right in on someone's property and assault 'em and slam 'em around like this, you wait till we complain to the state troopers. We bought this property, and we paid for it out of our own money that we earned at—well, we earned it all fair and square—"

"You never earned a penny in your lives," said Freddy. "Everything you've ever had you've stolen. You said you'd bought this property with the money you earned. Expect us to believe that?"

"Well, we did. You get this big bully to let me up and I'll show you the paper we've got to prove it. Then maybe you'll get out of here."

Leo glanced at Freddy, who nodded, and

The big paw shot out like lightning.

then he released Ezra. The rat hurried down the stairs and was back in a minute with a paper which he spread out on the ground. "This is the deed to this property," he said, "and it wouldn't do you any good to steal it or tear it up, because it is copied and recorded in Centerboro."

"H'm," said Freddy, as he read. " 'This indenture . . . H. Garble, party of the first part, and one Simon, a rat, party of the second part, witnesseth' . . . m'm, yes . . . 'in consideration of one dollar, paid by the party of the second part, and other good and lawful' . . . yes, seems to be correct . . . 'all that lot and parcel of land known as the Big Woods' . . . yes, and here's Garble's signature, properly witnessed, at the bottom. Well, I must say," Freddy remarked, turning to his friends, "that it seems in order." He nodded his head thoughtfully. "Yes, we'll have to think this over. Because," he continued, looking hard at Ezra, "if you think for one minute that Mr. Bean is going to allow a robber band to live right across the road from his farm, you're mistaken. Personally, I don't think the New York state law will allow a rat to own property. But even if it does—well, let's just say that I don't think you'll be very happy here."

"You sure won't," Jinx said. "All this

burned-over piece of woods—my goodness, it's so black there could be forty black cats sitting out here within a few feet of the house and you wouldn't see 'em at all. But there won't be forty black cats—there'll be just one, watching, waiting, creeping around night and day, waiting to JUMP!" With the last word he leaped at Ezra and, holding him down, started to tickle him. "Where'd you get the money to buy this place, hey? Answer me and I'll quit."

"Oh—yow!" Ezra squealed "Hee, hee, hee! Quit!"

Jinx paused. "Ain't got the nice clear tenor Simon has," he said to Freddy. "Upper register's very weak. I miss those clear bell-like tones his old man gives out with when you stick a claw into him—here." He scrabbled with his paw at the rat's side, and as Ezra wriggled and squealed: "How about it—where'd you get the money?" he demanded.

But Ezra only continued to screech and giggle, and Freddy said. "Let him go, Jinx. I know where Simon got it. Come on; we can't do anything more here."

Leo said in an undertone: "But aren't we going down cellar and clean 'em out?"

Freddy shook his head. "Too many tough fighters. It would be a lot worse than your

Uncle Ajax's goblins. Anyway, it wouldn't solve our problem."

As they walked back down to the farm, Freddy said: "You see, we've got to get Mr. Boom out of trouble first. We mustn't do anything that will give anyone the faintest suspicion that the Martians are rats. What we've got to do is get rid of them, but never let anybody guess what they are."

"But as long as the chief and all the public think they're Martians, they'll stay with the show," Leo objected.

"I think we can get around that," said Freddy. He glanced at his two friends. They were staring at him, puzzled, giving him, he thought, an unusually respectful attention. So he at once put on his Great Detective expression. It is a hard expression to describe. He shoved his jaw out determinedly, and he tried to make his eyes as piercing and hawklike as possible—something that is not easy for a pig, whose features are arranged on a different plan. But he did come close to something which was a sort of combination of George Washington and Winston Churchill.

"This case," he said, "is one of the strangest of my entire career. Usually it is my task to solve some crime, to uncover all the facts, to track down the evildoer, and to bring him to justice. But here it is just the other way round. We know all the facts, we have tracked down the evildoer—and now we have to keep the facts covered up and protect the criminal. Truly a strange task for a skilled detective. However—"

"Look, pig," said Jinx, who was getting tired of the eloquence, "just skip all the salted nuts and little pink candies. What are you going to *do?*"

"Well, the setup's this," Freddy said. "Somehow or other, Garble got in touch with Simon and fixed up this Martian business. Or maybe Simon thought it up; he's got better brains than Garble. They put on their flying-saucer stunt at Lanksburg, because the circus was there, and it was almost a certainty that when Mr. Boom heard about Martians landing, almost next door, he'd try to get them for his circus. Well, we don't know what kind of a deal the rats made with Garble, but they must have split the money they took in, and he must have agreed to buy the Big Woods for them."

"But why would they want the Big Woods?" Jinx asked.

"They lived for a long time at the Bean farm," Freddy said. "Several times they've come back, when they knew we'd drive 'em out and they could just as well have settled somewhere else. They have always wanted to get even with us, and with the Beans, for chasing them away, and my hunch is, they think they can make a deal to get back in the barn. Maybe they really think they can drive the Beans out. They tried it once before, you know—and they did drive that Mrs. Filmore out of her hotel, with the help of Mr. Eha, remember? And you know, with money behind them, and with Garble's help, they might get away with it. They've been planning it for years.

"But I've got an idea. Come on down to my study and talk it over."

So they went down and talked it over all the rest of the afternoon. They changed it some, then after supper they called a meeting of all the animals in the barn and Freddy made a speech.

First, he outlined the situation, and when everybody agreed that they must protect Mr. Boomschmidt, even if it meant putting off trying to get rid of the rats, he said: "Now I have an idea how all this can be done. And I am going to call upon a group of animals whose record of patriotism and courage is known to all of you. I am going to call upon them to come for-

ward and offer their services in helping to get
rid of the rats. I call upon the Horrible Ten
to come forward."

The Horrible Ten was a club composed entirely of rabbits. They had been organized first
as a joke, when they wanted to scare some of
the larger animals. With their ears tied down
to disguise themselves, and brandishing glittering little tin knives, they would lie in wait at
night and then rush out and dance a sort of war
dance around their victims, brandishing their
knives and chanting a bloodthirsty song. Evidently they were prepared for something of
the kind this evening, for when Freddy called
on them they came out and went into their
dance in the middle of the barn floor.

"We are the Horrible Ten, [they sang]
We've warned you again and again.
We've warned you by letter, we've warned you
*   by phone.*
If you want to dodge trouble just leave us alone.
For our appetite's good, and our favorite food
Is someone like you, either baked, boiled, or
*   stewed.*
So beware and take care and don't get in our
*   hair,*
Or you may find your name on next week's bill
*   of fare."*

There was enthusiastic applause at the end of the dance, and then Freddy said: "Thank you, gentlemen, that was very nice. And now I would like one volunteer for a duty which may be dangerous. Will one of you step forward?"

The Horribles stepped forward as one rabbit.

"Very well," said Freddy, as the applause from the audience fairly shook the roof, "I had expected nothing less. But I think, then, that Rabbit No. 23 should be selected. He is, I believe, the Head Horrible, is he not?"

No. 23 stepped forward. "I am ready," he said simply.

"Good," said Freddy, just as simply. "And now, ladies and gentlemen, I will tell you what we propose to do."

CHAPTER

11

Late that night Freddy and Jinx and Leo and Rabbit No. 23 entered the circus grounds. They had hitched up Hank and driven to Centerboro in their old phaeton, instead of having Mr. Hercules drive them back, because they didn't want Mr. Boomschmidt to know what they were up to. No. 23 had on a red suit like those the Martians wore. It was one of six that Mrs.

Bean had made for Freddy out of an old suit of Mr. Bean's red flannel underwear. And Freddy had made some luxuriant red whiskers out of a silk tassel off one of Mrs. Bean's sofa pillows.

The nice thing about Mrs. Bean, when you wanted her to do something, was that she didn't ask a lot of questions. She said: "You want these suits just like the ones the Martians wear, is that right?" And Freddy said: "Yes. But we'd rather not say why we want 'em."

Mrs. Bean laughed. "All right, then, I won't ask. And I guess you don't want me to tell anybody about it, do you?"

"Oh, you could tell Mr. Bean. But we don't want Mr. Boom or Mr. Garble to find out. That would be bad for everybody."

Mrs. Bean said: "You're making me pretty curious."

Freddy said he'd tell her the whole story as soon as he could.

At the circus grounds they crept quietly in close to the Martian tent, then No. 23 and Jinx went inside and 23 climbed up and went in the little door at the end of the cage. There were electric lights strung around the grounds, so that it wasn't entirely dark in the tent, and 23 could see that five of the little beds were occupied, and that the sixth, which must be Simon's, was empty. On the peg above it hung the little red nightshirt and nightcap, and he tiptoed across and took them down. Then, moving as quietly as he could, he got out of his red suit and into the nightshirt, and crawled into bed.

But something had awakened the Martian in the next bed. He sat up and peered hard at 23. "Is that you, Granddad?" he whispered.

"Your granddad sent me to take his place," the rabbit replied. "He had to stay at the Grimby house."

Another Martian woke up. "What's going on here?" he demanded. "Who's this guy?"

In a minute more all five of them were crowding around his bed, asking who he was and why Simon had sent a stranger to take his place, instead of one of his own family. There was not enough light for them to see that he wasn't a rat, but he knew that they'd spot him in the daylight, so he said: "None of your family could come; that's why Simon sent me."

"Why couldn't they come?" one asked.

"Oh, how do I know?" said 23 crossly. "I'm just telling you what Simon said." He started to sit up, but in doing so knocked off his nightcap and disarranged his red whiskers.

"Holy smoke! A rabbit!" a rat exclaimed.

"Hey, Zeke, we can't have this guy in here, can we?"

Zeke was Simon's oldest son. He was evidently in charge in his father's absence. "Yeah, we can keep him," he said. "We do need someone in Father's place. But maybe we can get some information out of him first. Hold him down, boys. Banjo, where are those pliers?"

No. 23 didn't like the sound of that at all. But Freddy, who knew the rats, had thought something of the kind might happen, and he had arranged for it with Jinx. The cat had followed 23 in and concealed himself behind the Martian dinner table. Now he suddenly pounced. He landed on Zeke, knocking the wind out of him. The other rats scattered, squeaking, into corners.

"Quiet, boys, quiet!" Jinx said. "You start a row and—well, I won't tickle you like I tickled your grandpa: too noisy. But I promise you, by tomorrow morning you'll be quiet, all right. Yes, sir; awful quiet, and laid out flat, side by side, with your poor little limp tails all tied together ready for Mr. Garble to pick you up and drop you in the trash can. Now you just hop right back between the sheets and go beddy-bye."

The rats hopped. And when they were all back in their beds, Jinx said: "Now I'm going to

stay right here, to see that you boys behave.
Right over here by the door, because I don't
want any of you to go wandering around and
getting lost."

"You can't keep us in here," said Zeke. "You
wait till Mr. Garble hears about this."

"He won't hear about it," Jinx said. "Because
the first one of you that tries to say a word to
Garble will get his little red suit all clawed to
pieces, and maybe his handsome gray hide
might get some rips in it, too. Also, anyone who
bothers this gentleman here who is taking the
place of your dear grandpa will get the same
treatment."

"You mean you're going to stay right here in
the cage?" said Zeke. "You can't get away with
it, cat. Come on, rabbit; you'd better go, and
take your bodyguard with you. You go quietly
and we'll just forget the whole thing."

But 23 wasn't scared, now that he had Jinx
with him. "Nothing doing," he said. "I stay
and so does the cat. If people ask questions,
you'll just say that Martians are fond of cats,
and on one of your walks you found this cat and
decided to keep him as a pet. The people will be
delighted. Can't you just hear them? 'How
sweet! What nice people the Martians must be!
And what a pretty pussy! Come, Kitty, come
little sweetums—' "

"That's enough," said Jinx. "Just lay off the sweetums, rabbit."

Zeke said: "You don't think Garble is going to be taken in by that kind of stuff, do you?"

"Who cares?" said Jinx. "Just don't try to explain anything to him, and let him think what he wants to." He sat up and let Zeke go. "Now come on, rat, and get into bed. Come on, my pretty; Uncle Jinxy will tuck you in." Which he insisted on doing, much to the rat's disgust. "Shall Uncle Jinxy kiss him good night?"

"Yah!" said Zeke, and burrowed down under the bedclothes.

Morning, of course, brought Mr. Garble, and with Jinx's yellow eyes on him, Zeke said his piece. This cat was an old friend; they had asked him to stay with them. Mr. Garble was puzzled, but made no objection. And when the people began filing through, and he saw how pleased they were that the Martians were fond of pets, he didn't say anything more.

Zeke, however, was a smart rat, and he very nearly managed to get rid of Jinx that first morning, for he remembered how the cat had teased him the night before. He'd wait until there was a good audience in front of the cage, and then he would call Jinx. "Come, kitty-kitty! Come, oo nice pussy-cat, oo!" He talked the most outrageous baby talk to him, and scratched his ears and patted him. "Just a precious ickle petty-lamb, so he is!" Jinx growled under his breath, but he didn't dare do anything about it. And at last he whispered to 23 that he just couldn't take any more. "I'm sorry," he said, "but the next time that guy pulls that gooey line I'm going to give him the old claws, right in his gizzard. You've got to get a new bodyguard; I can't take it."

"You don't go at it right," said 23. "Look, when somebody pulls a line on you that you don't like, you can't get anywhere by getting mad, or by arguing. Particularly when you can't fight. And you can't fight now. But we rabbits aren't fighters anyway, and there's one way we've learned to handle such things. Don't argue, don't oppose the fellow; agree with him. Take it right up and carry it on farther than he does. If he's sticky sweet to you, you be stickier and sweeter to him. Do you get it?"

Jinx thought about it for a while; then he began to grin. And the next time Zeke called him, he went right over and began to purr. "Oh, oo tunnin' ittle kitty-witty, oo," said Zeke. "Wants his ittle ears scratched." He reached out a red-gloved paw towards the cat's head. And Jinx turned quickly and rubbed his cheek against the rat's face. He was of course twice as big as Zeke, who was pushed right off balance; and immedi-

"Come, kitty-kitty!"

ately he rubbed his other cheek against Zeke's shoulder. Zeke fell over on the floor.

Then Jinx, purring as loudly as he could, did as No. 23 had advised: he showed exaggerated affection for the rat. He rubbed against him, pushing him all over the cage, and he got him down and kneaded him with his forepaws, taking care not to let his claws go far enough in to make the rat squeal. Then he licked him affectionately on the face until the red whiskers were limp, and Zeke was practically crying with anger and embarrassment, while the audience roared with laughter, and even the other Martians had to hide their faces in their pillows.

That was the end of any attempt to get rid of Jinx. After that the rats let him alone. All that day he stayed on guard. After the show that evening Zeke and the rat called Banjo came towards the little door. "We're just going out for a stroll," Zeke said, in a careless tone.

"Oh no you're not," Jinx replied. "From now on no more evening strolls." He curled up in front of the door. "If you need exercise, my little popsy-wopsies," he said, "you stroll around the cage. And if you'll excuse me, I'll just take forty winks." He closed his eyes. "But remember," he said sharply, "first one that tries to get past me gets scalped."

None of them tried.

CHAPTER

12

Along about midnight there was a faint scratching at the little door in the Martian cage. Jinx, who was sleeping right against it, got up and opened it. Another member of the Horrible Ten, Rabbit No. 34, dressed in a red suit, came quietly in. And after him about six feet of Willy came smoothly gliding. The snake's head swayed for a moment above the row of little beds, then darted down quickly. He picked up the rat called Banjo by the head and shoulders, snaked him out from under the covers before he could squeak once, and the next thing Banjo knew, he was in a wire rat-trap under an old blanket in a dark corner of Willy's cage. And No. 34 had slipped into his bed.

It was of course Freddy's plan to turn all the rat-Martians into rabbit-Martians without Mr. Garble's knowledge. Then if they could all disappear some night, leaving a note saying that their friends had come for them and they had gone back to Mars, Mr. Boomschmidt's reputation would be saved, and Mr. Garble couldn't say a word.

This evening Freddy had left his plan in charge of Leo and Willy and Jinx and the Horribles, and they worked so quietly that by morning there were five rats crowded into the trap in Willy's cage, and six Horribles in the little red nightshirts—which were much too small for them—sleeping more or less peacefully in the Martian cage. But Freddy was in trouble.

After he had arranged the plan of substituting Horribles for Martians, Freddy had had to go to Mr. Weezer's for supper. He would much rather have stayed and supervised the operation, but the invitation had been given nearly a week before, and as Mr. Weezer was President of the Centerboro Bank, and as Freddy was also a bank official (he was President of the First Animal), it was not an invitation that could be lightly disregarded. Then too, Freddy thought that he might be able to get some information about the sale of the Big Woods to the rats.

The talk at the supper table was mostly about banking and money matters. Freddy had to be careful, however, for Mr. Weezer had a peculiarity which is not uncommon among bankers—at the mention of any sum larger than ten dollars his glasses fell off. Freddy had to regulate his conversation so that Mr. Weezer's glasses were never in danger of falling into soup, or any squashy vegetable, or ice cream. Occasionally, in order not to have too long pauses in the conversation, Freddy would give a word of warning; he would say, for instance: "I believe that Mr. Billgus sent a check for— please hold onto your glasses—eighteen dollars."

Mr. Weezer did know that Mr. Margarine had sold the Big Woods to Mr. Garble. He was not at liberty, of course, to reveal the exact sum which Mr. Garble had paid, but confidentially it was in the neighborhood—the near neighborhood—of three hundred dollars. Of any subsequent transaction with the rats, however, he knew nothing. "Wouldn't the payment have been made through the Animal Bank, rather than through mine?" he asked.

"No rat has ever been allowed to open an account in the First Animal," Freddy said. "No doubt they paid cash." He didn't tell Mr. Weezer what he suspected—that the rats had been given the house in return for pretending to be Martians.

They had just finished supper when there was a knock on the front door. Mrs. Weezer went. There was no one there, but on the floor was a soiled slip of paper. She brought it in. "This seems to be for you," she said, and handed it to Freddy. Written on it in pencil, in a very shaky hand, was this message: "Freddy. As long as Marshans are Marshans chickins will be chickins, when Marshans are not Marshans chickins will be et, so kepe your big mouth shut brother." There was no signature.

Freddy knew what it meant, but he couldn't tell the Weezers, so he pretended to puzzle over it and then put it in his pocket. "Probably from one of the rabbits who do detective work for me," he said, and quickly turned the conversation to some of his recent cases.

As soon as he could, he got away. He had rather expected something like this note. It was

There was no signature.

plain now that the rats had Chiquita and Little Broiler. The threat to eat them if Freddy didn't keep his mouth shut about who the Martians really were was plain. Freddy could have laughed at it, for he was just as unwilling to unmask the Martians as Mr. Garble was. But he had worried a lot about the chickens. And now the chances seemed to be that they were held captive either at the Grimby house, or at the mansion of Mr. Garble's sister, Mrs. Underdunk, where Mr. Garble was staying while the circus was in Centerboro.

So first Freddy went to see his friend the sheriff, who ran the jail. The sheriff knew all about the law, and Freddy asked him if there would be trouble if the Bean animals went in force and threw the rats out of the Grimby house.

The sheriff looked in a lot of his law books, but he couldn't find anything about rats owning property. "And as long as it don't say they can't," he said, "why, that's the same as sayin' they can, ain't it? It's like if you wanted, say, to climb a telegraph pole. As long as there ain't any law that says: 'it is hereby declared illegal for pigs to climb telegraph poles,' well then, you got a perfect right to climb one whenever you feel like it.

"Of course," the sheriff went on, "there may

be some law I don't know about. Lots of times there's little unimportant laws get passed, and my goodness, you can't even find 'em in the index. And you go along, thinking you're minding your own business, and then bang! you trip over one of 'em, and you're in a peck of trouble.

"So then you got those rats owning the Grimby house, and if you go in there and throw 'em out, they can have you arrested for assault and battery, burglary, snooping, and I don't know what all."

After this, it didn't seem to Freddy that it would be a very good idea to try to get the rats out of the Grimby house now. For even if it turned out that rats weren't allowed to own property, Mr. Garble, who had sold them the house, would be the owner in the eyes of the law, and he would be just as pleased to have Freddy arrested as Simon would. So Freddy said: "Is Red Mike still in jail? Could I borrow him for a while this evening?"

Red Mike was an ex-burglar—at least he was an ex-burglar as long as he was in jail—because, although the prisoners were allowed to go out calling in the evening, or to the movies, Mike had promised not to do any burgling in Centerboro until his jail sentence had expired.

"Mike's giving a little talk over in the assembly hall right now," the sheriff said. "It's one of a series of lectures we've arranged."

"That's something new, isn't it?" Freddy asked.

"Yes, some of the folks in town thought the prisoners were having too much fun, playing games and going to movies and so on; they thought they ought to be getting some education. Most of 'em ain't had much schoolin'. I haven't, myself, and I must say these talks are real instructive."

"What's Mike talking about?"

"Practical burgling. How to get in doors and windows from the outside. And if he has time, he's going to talk about going upstairs without waking folks up. We've had some real good lectures. Only one wasn't so successful was Looey's talk on safe-cracking. I let him use my office safe to demonstrate with, and he blew the door off the hinges. No place where I can lock up my records now. Though, as a matter of fact, I've always kept 'em in my head. And I dunno as you'd find much if you blew the door off that. Well, let's go over and hear the rest of his talk."

There were ten or fifteen prisoners and a sprinkling of townspeople in the assembly hall, and Red Mike was up on the platform. He was showing them his kit of burglar tools and explaining how each one worked. "Though a good burglar," he said, "he don't need no fancy tools. Take this here padlock." He held it up. "You don't need no key to open it; hit it a crack right here with a hammer, and she flies right open." He demonstrated. "And there's other locks you can open the same way. Only I don't recommend no such method, unless the folks in the house is deaf. You can't go banging on the front door with a hammer if you're plannin' to steal the table silver." He glanced at his wrist watch. "Well, I see my time's nearly up. Any questions?"

"Is it your opinion, Mr.—Mr. Mike," asked an elderly lady, "that it is true what they say— that crime does not pay?"

"Ma'am," said Mike, "I am very happy to express myself on that topic. No ma'am, crime does not pay, unless you get caught. And I will enlarge on that statement, ma'am. I never had three square meals a day when I was burgling. And I was so nervous that I couldn'ta et 'em if I had. 'Twasn't till I got caught and sent to jail that I could eat good and enjoy myself. Now the county pays for my food, and the sheriff here sees to my entertainment. Of course I can't stay here forever. But when my time's up— well, maybe I'll try to pry the door off the bank and get sent back again. It sure is a nice jail,

ma'am. You ought to put a rock through somebody's front window and try it for a day or
two."

"Now, now, Mike," said the sheriff reprovingly, "the jail don't need any free advertising.
It's full up,—not an empty room for another
month. Come down, here's Freddy wants a
word with you."

Freddy didn't have much trouble persuading
Mike to help him burgle the Underdunk house.
The burglar had no use for Mr. Garble, who
had once tried to do the sheriff out of his job,
and he had even less use for Mrs. Underdunk,
who a year or so before had headed a committee
of citizens who had investigated the jail. Their
report, published in the paper, stated, among
other things, that Mike's room was untidy. This
had made Mike sore. Of course, his room really
was untidy. If it hadn't been, he wouldn't have
minded.

Fortunately, Mike didn't have to hammer on
any of the Underdunk locks or smash any of the
Underdunk windows. A pantry window was unlocked, and they got in without any trouble,
though Mike knocked a small pitcher off the
shelf and fell over a chair as they were going
through the kitchen. However, there were no
sounds from upstairs, so, having found the cellar door, they started down the stairs, because

the cellar seemed the likeliest place to look for the kidnapped chickens.

"Didn't get to the part in my lecture about stairs," Mike whispered. "But I'll show you about 'em, now. Thing to avoid is squeaks. And if you step on the inside, like this, close to the wall, you hardly ever get squeaks. Squeaks is mostly in the middle of a step. Squeaks—"

But Freddy never found out what more there was to say about squeaks, for at this point Mike slipped, his flashlight flew out of his hand, his feet flew out from under him, he grabbed at Freddy, and the two of them went crashing and banging, over and over each other, down the whole flight to the hard concrete cellar floor. And as they lay there trying to sort out their arms and legs from the tangle, there was a shout and a pounding of heavy feet upstairs, and before they could even get up, the light flashed on, and Mr. Garble, with a large pistol in his hand, was looking down at them from the top of the stairs.

CHAPTER
13

It was that same day that a real flying saucer,
with real Martians in it, landed. A strange coincidence, some thought, that it should land on
the outskirts of Centerboro. For here, within a
radius of a few miles, were the Martian side
show, Uncle Ben's space ship, and a flying saucer

from Mars. But it really was no coincidence, as it turned out.

The saucer landed, without any fuss, in a vacant lot not far from the circus grounds. There was no roaring sound and no flare of light; it came in, rotating slowly, and settled gently on the grass; then a hatch in the top opened and four or five spidery little creatures climbed out.

Uncle Ben was taking Mrs. Peppercorn home after her day's work on the rocket, and they were the only witnesses—which was perhaps fortunate. Uncle Ben stopped the station wagon, and they stared for a moment. "Well!" said Mrs. Peppercorn. "Wonder where *they're* from! Not from Mars, if those critters Garble's showing are Martians—which I beg leave to doubt."

Uncle Ben just grunted.

"Well, don't just sit there!" said the old lady crossly, starting to climb out. "Let's see what they've got to say for themselves. I guess they ain't Rooshians, anyway. Leastways, ain't any Rooshians I ever heard of that had four arms."

Rather unwillingly, Uncle Ben followed her. The strangers were certainly queer looking. They were black, with round bodies and four black spindly arms; they were about two feet high and had long feelers on their heads. Seen by the watery light of a sliver of new moon, they were not reassuring as they turned and came to meet the humans. For they took some getting used to, as Mrs. Peppercorn later remarked.

> *"I'd have to get used t' em*
> *Before I'd troost 'em,"*

she said.

But she went straight towards them. A little thing like a group of visitors from outer space never bothered Mrs. Peppercorn.

Seen closer, they were even more queer looking. They had three round, lidless eyes, two of which looked at you, while the third and middle one rolled around independently as if keeping watch for possible enemies. They had no necks; their heads were pear-shaped and set close to their bodies. They walked upright; they were not exactly spidery, and yet they reminded you more of spiders than of anything else.

She went forward, holding out her hand. "How de do," she said. "And where might you be from?"

While they didn't understand her speech, they must have known what an earth-person's first question would be, for the one who was apparently the leader pointed to the sky with

But she went straight towards them.

one hand. Then he took her hand in two of his and looked at it carefully. The other crowded round him, talking some sort of language which was all clicks and squeaks. Then he passed her hand around and they all examined it.

She looked at Uncle Ben. "Think likely they're going to tell my fortune?" she asked. "Great on holdin' hands, these little fellers."

Uncle Ben squatted down on the ground and began drawing with a stick. He drew the sun, then around it the orbits of the planets. The spider-men watched intently. When he drew the orbit of Mars and put that planet in with a jab of the stick, they clicked and squeaked excitedly, and the leader's gesture was unmistakable—pointing first to Uncle Ben's picture of Mars, then to himself, then to the sky.

"Martians," said Uncle Ben. "*Real* ones," he added. "Garble—phooey!"

Then he pointed to himself, to Mrs. Peppercorn, and to his picture of the earth. Whereupon the Martians waved their feelers rapidly backward and forward—which was evidently equivalent to a vigorous nod of assent. For, as Mrs. Peppercorn said:

> *"When your head and your neck*
> *Are so closely connec-*

ted, you can't nod or shake,
It's a serious defeck."

This, she admitted frankly, was not one of her best efforts, but she was, of course, pretty excited at the time.

Uncle Ben pointed to himself and said: "Benjamin Bean"; then to Mrs. Peppercorn, and named her. The head Martian pointed to himself and gave what sounded like two clicks. Then he pointed to the others and named them in succession. Of course, without a Martian alphabet, and without the ability to pronounce it even if they had it, the two humans could only speak of their visitors as Two-clicks, Squeakclick, Three-squeaks, and so on.

Then Two-clicks took the stick and drew on the ground a picture which Uncle Ben recognized as his rocket ship. It would take too long to describe all the drawings and gestures by which Uncle Ben and Two-clicks managed to understand each other. Perhaps nobody but Uncle Ben could have understood the Martian, or have made him understand. As a person who never said more than one word when anybody else would have needed a hundred, Uncle Ben was pretty good at sign language. And when he learned that they wanted to see the space ship, which they apparently knew about, he invited them to visit it; and the upshot was that he and Mrs. Peppercorn got into the saucer with them and whirled up to the Big Woods. Two-clicks even let Mrs. Peppercorn steer it part of the way.

So the Martians inspected the space ship, and Uncle Ben and Mrs. Peppercorn inspected the flying saucer, and by the time that was over, the sun stood a good foot above the horizon. Neither of the two was sleepy, and the Martians apparently weren't interested in sleep either, so Uncle Ben invited them down to meet Mr. and Mrs. Bean. They accepted—probably without much idea of what they were going to see, but of course everything on earth was of interest to them.

Mrs. Bean was up and just taking the coffee off the stove when she looked out the window and saw Uncle Ben and Mrs. Peppercorn coming through the barnyard, accompanied by some of the strangest creatures she had ever seen. Two-clicks, who seemed to have taken a great fancy to Mrs. Peppercorn, was walking hand in hand with her—at least three of his hands were holding onto one of hers. What Mrs. Bean thought, goodness only knows, but all she said was: "Come here, Mr. B. Company coming. Suppose we'll have to ask 'em to breakfast."

Mr. Bean came and looked out. "By cracky," he said, "I always thought Uncle Ben had some pretty queer friends, but these beat 'em all! They're kind of spidery looking; think I'd better catch a few flies?"

Breakfast, however, went off pretty well, although Mr. Bean had to fetch nearly all the books in the bookcase for the guests to sit upon, so they could get up to the table. Squeak-squeak burned himself on the coffee, and Mr. Bean had a hard time not to laugh when he put all four hands up and waved them in front of his mouth. But Mrs. Bean quickly poured him some cold water, and he rolled his third eye at her gratefully.

Now what they would have done with their guests after this I don't know, but fortunately Mr. and Mrs. Webb came into the kitchen. They were elderly spiders who had been with the Beans for a long time, in charge of flies. The morning was chilly in the parlor, and they walked in across the ceiling to stand upside down above the coal range and warm themselves. And Two-clicks caught sight of them.

Instantly he jumped up, and the other Martians jumped up, too, and there was a great clicking and squeaking; and then, to the humans' amazement, the Webbs came spinning down on a strand of cobweb and landed on

Two-click's shoulder. The Martian put his feelers down and touched them, and then began talking very fast in his queer language. He would talk for a bit, and then wait, as if for a reply, while the other Martians crowded closer. This went on for some time. The humans couldn't hear the Webbs' voices, but apparently they were talking, and being understood.

After a while Mrs. Webb jumped down onto the table and ran up Mrs. Bean's sleeve to her shoulder, and spoke into her ear. She was a little afraid of Mr. Bean, but she was fond of Mrs. Bean—partly because they looked a little alike—being round and plump, with a merry expression, though Mrs. Webb wore a bang and Mrs. Bean's hair was pulled straight back.

"We can understand 'em," the spider said. "They're from Mars all right, and somehow they heard that some circus had captured some Martians and was showing them in a cage, for money. Naturally they didn't like this, and that's why they're here—they came to rescue them. I told them what Mr. Garble's Martians looked like, and they didn't understand it, but they want to go see them."

"But how on earth can you talk to them?" Mrs. Bean asked.

"It's a little too long to tell you now," Mrs. Webb said, "and I don't know that I under-

stand it exactly, either. They've really developed from the same kind of people that we
spiders developed from. Just the way you people developed from monkeys. They developed
one way and we developed another. I don't
know how they got to Mars. But it's the old
spider language we're talking—Webb and I
learned it when we were little. It's like Latin in
your schools. All educated spiders understand
it."

"Gracious," said Mrs. Bean, "I had Latin in
school, but I don't remember a word of it
now."

"Well," Mrs. Webb said, "these people still
talk it. I suppose it sounds queer to you, but it's
wonderful to us to hear it again. My, my, how
it takes me back!"

When all this had been explained to the
other humans, the Martians, who were anxious
to get to the circus grounds, invited the Beans to
ride with them in the flying saucer. Rather to
Mr. Bean's surprise, Mrs. Bean accepted at
once.

"Well, then, I'm a-comin' too," said Mr.
Bean. "We'll likely end whizzin' round the
Milky Way for the next million years, but if
you was to go without me, and get back safe, I
guess I'd never hear the last of it. Lead on
there, Clickety What's-your-name."

The saucer had a sort of conning tower on top, with a doorway through which they all climbed. Inside, it was roomy and comfortably furnished, with plush settees around the sides, and a big table to which a number of strange things were clamped. It was really very cozy when the hatch was closed and Two-clicks, with a twist of a lever, set the saucer in motion. It rose, whirling slowly, then leveled off, and Two-clicks said something to Mrs. Bean.

Mrs. Webb spoke in her ear. "The captain wants to know if you wouldn't like to take the —the tiller, I suppose you'd call it. Thing you steer with. He says maybe you'd enjoy taking a little run up and around over Syracuse before steering for the circus grounds. Says he'd like to have you steer."

Mrs. Bean put her hands up to her mouth. "My land!" she said. "My land!" Then she slid her eyes around towards her husband. Good grief, Mr. B., do you think I ought . . . Why, I ain't ever even driven a car!"

Mr. Bean smiled reassuringly at her. "Go ahead, Mrs. B.," he said. "Guess you've steered me without scrapin' any of the paint off for the past forty years; guess you can steer a little simple contraption like this one. Go ahead."

So Mrs. Bean, looking out through the little window where the steeples of Centerboro were now visible ahead, seized the tiller firmly and swung it over. The saucer dipped, turned, and headed for Syracuse. For a moment, however, she hesitated. For she remembered suddenly that she had left the pan of johnnycake in the oven. It would be burned to a cinder. Then she put all thought of the johnnycake out of her mind. She giggled delightedly. And then she began to sing.

CHAPTER

14

While all this was going on, Freddy and Red
Mike were sitting on the cold floor of Mrs. Underdunk's cellar. They had been locked into a
closet stocked with hundreds of cans of jam.
The door was not solid, but was made of a sort
of grill of heavy strips of wood, and fastened
by a big padlock. Mr. Garble had made Mike

give up his kit of burglar tools before locking him in, but he hadn't searched his prisoner, who had a small flashlight, about as big as a pencil, taped to his forearm. This he got out and began examining their prison.

"If I was outside I could open that padlock," said Mike.

"How about thinking of something that you *can* do?" Freddy replied. "Garble will have the troopers here before long, and then we'll be in real trouble."

"We can bust the door down," Mike replied. "But it would be too noisy. Guess we'll have to saw those crosspieces out."

"If you had a saw," said Freddy wearily.

Mike said: "Look." He rolled up his sleeve. There was a hacksaw blade taped to his arm. "Never know when things like that will come in handy, even in jail," he said.

"Did the sheriff know about it?" Freddy asked.

"Sure thing. I got the tape from him . . . Well, let's get to work." Holding the ends of the little blade between the forefingers and thumbs of each hand, he began sawing one of the crossbars.

"You go so slow," said Freddy. "You'll never get through it."

"If we go faster, Garble will hear it and

come down," Mike said; and when Freddy objected that Garble could certainly hear it anyway, Mike said: "Look. You saw at just the same rate you breathe in and out. Don't you see what it sounds like?"

"Sounds like somebody sawing, to me," said the pig.

"It sounds like somebody snorin', stupid. Even if Garble comes down, when he opens the door I stop sawing and give a kind of snort and sit up and say: 'Who's there?' Fools him every time."

It did sound a little like somebody snoring. Unfortunately, Mr. Garble had quietly opened the door at the head of the stairs while they were still talking, and he snapped the light on before Mike could hide the saw blade and pretend to wake up with a snort. Five minutes later Mr. Garble had gone back upstairs, and Mike and Freddy were lying side by side on the floor, tied up with clothesline.

Mike was discouraged. "I wish I was back in jail," he said. "I always get in trouble if I leave jail."

"Look," said Freddy, "there's a jackknife in my coat pocket. See if you can roll over so you can get your hand in and open it."

Mike managed it after a while. He got the knife and cut Freddy loose. When they were both free, Freddy said: "We can't cut our way out with this knife. But I've got an idea. Maybe it will work and maybe not, but we've got to try it, because these Garbles, they'd shoot you as soon as look at you if they thought they could get away with it. And they could. They'd just say they caught us breaking into the house. So now look—this is what we'll do."

He had not finished explaining, however, when a voice from somewhere in the cellar said: "Freddy! Is that you?"

Freddy was silent for a minute, then he said cautiously: "Yes. Who is it?"

"It's me—Chiquita. I wasn't sure it was you, before. We're in a sort of cage over by the coal bin. Broiler is with me, and Mrs. Hapgood."

"Who is Mrs. Hapgood?" Freddy asked.

"Why, she's a prisoner here, too. She can whistle 'Dixie,' and Mr. Garble got her to come here because he said he was going to start a circus, and wanted her for his star act." There were some whispered cluckings, and then Chiquita said: "Oh, excuse me. Mrs. Hapgood, this is Mr. Freddy."

"How do you do, I'm sure," said a very affected voice which Freddy took to be that of the talented hen.

"Very happy," said Freddy politely. "Let me present my friend, Mr. Mike."

"How ja do," said Mrs. Hapgood distantly. She evidently didn't like having burglars introduced to her. Then she said: "Mr. Freddy, can you do anything to get me out of this dreadful place? I understood I was to be a star, playing before large audiences, but here I am locked in this horrid damp cellar for weeks, with no company but that of these two children. It's not the sort of thing I'm used to, Mr. Freddy."

"I'm sure it's not," said Freddy. "Chiquita, are you and Little Broiler all right?"

"I am," said the chicken. "Broiler has got a cold."

"And no handkerchief, I bet," Freddy said. "He's had that cold as long as I've known him."

"Well, I can't help it if I got the sniffles," Broiler complained. "I'm sick. I wanna go home." And he began to wail.

"Oh, stop *whining!*" said Freddy. "We'll get you out of here if we can."

Mrs. Hapgood said: "He's not very cheerful company. That Mr. Garble sent out and got him and his sister to be company for me. That was after I'd told him I had no intention of staying here in the dark all alone until he got his circus started. But this young one does nothing but snivel from morning till night."

"Garble says he got them to be company for you, does he?" Freddy said. "Well, he had another reason, too. But we're wasting time. Sit tight and let's see if we can't get out of here."

So then Freddy opened a big jar of strawberry jam. He smeared a lot on the front of Mike's shirt, and when Mike lay down on his back close to the door, he poured out the juice so it ran out under the door and made a little red pool on the floor. And then when they were all ready, Mike began to yell at the top of his lungs: "Help! Murder!" And then he topped off with a screech that could have been heard a mile.

Feet pounded overhead, the door flew open, and Mr. Garble, pistol in hand, snapped on the cellar light and dashed down the stairs. He saw the strawberry juice trickling out from under the door; looking in through the slats, he saw Freddy sitting astride Mike, flourishing a knife. Mike was just moaning weakly now, and fluttering his eyelids rapidly. He had an idea that this indicated that he was just about gone.

Mrs. Underdunk, in a black dressing gown with gold dragons on it, was just behind her brother. "Shoot, Herb! Shoot that pig!" she exclaimed. "You'll never get a better chance."

Freddy hadn't thought about the possibility of being shot; his tail became completely un-

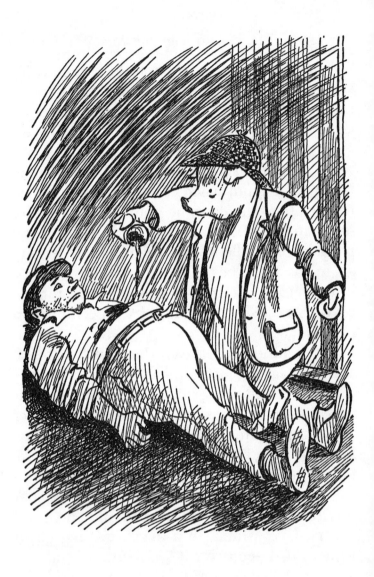

He poured out a lot of juice.

curled, and he felt something like a procession of ants with very cold feet walking up his spine.

But Mr. Garble said: "No. No shooting. Much better to let Uncle Orville have him. That way he'll just disappear and nobody'll know. And Uncle Orville can have some good fat bacon for breakfast."

So he lowered the pistol and began to unlock the door. "Get Smith," he said over his shoulder to his sister. "We'll have to get this guy to a hospital."

When the chauffeur had come and Mike had been carried up the cellar stairs, Mr. Garble went down and locked Freddy in again. "We'll have a talk with you later," he said menacingly. Then he returned to the kitchen where, having sent Mrs. Underdunk to phone for a doctor, he had left Mike lying on the floor, watched over by Smith. And he got an unpleasant surprise. For now Smith was lying on the floor and Mike had vanished.

Smith opened his eyes and sat up dazedly, just as Mrs. Underdunk came back.

"The doctor will be here—" she began, then broke off. "Why, this is Smith!"

"He struck me," said Smith, feeling of his nose. "Almost dead, he was, and he jumped up and socked me!"

Mrs. Underdunk stood staring at him for a

moment. "You're a fool, Smith," she said. "Look at this." She bent and pointed to two strawberries which had fallen off Mike's shirt. "Jam. You're a bright pair, I must say. I'll go tell the doctor not to come."

"But maybe Smith needs him," said Mr. Garble.

Mrs. Underdunk said sharply: "If you think I'm going to pay out my good money for him, you're greatly mistaken. He can pay for his own doctor. Maybe it'll teach him not to let himself get punched in the nose." She glared at her brother.

Mr. Garble said: "I know who Mike is. He's one of the prisoners at the jail. I'll have to go head him off before he gets back there and tells the sheriff, or the sheriff will come up here and make us release Freddy. They're great friends."

"He can't make us release a burglar," his sister snapped.

"No, but he can arrest him and take him to the jail. And then he'll be tried. Maybe you want to hear what he will say when he comes to trial, but I don't."

"No," said Mrs. Underdunk thoughtfully, "I don't either. You'd better go."

Then, when her brother had gone, she went and stood over the chauffeur, who was sitting up and trying to wiggle his nose. "Get up, Smith," she said harshly. "Go get that crate from the barn—I know we've still got it—and put that pig in it and ship it to my Uncle Orville as soon as the express office opens in the morning."

Locked in the jam closet in the cellar, Freddy groaned. He had heard Mrs. Underdunk, and he knew that crate. It was the one in which he had been packed up once before, for shipment to Mr. Garble's uncle, who had a stock farm in Montana. "And this time," he said to himself, "it looks as if I was going to get there."

CHAPTER
15

Mr. Garble didn't overtake Mike before he got to the jail. But Mike had lost his latchkey, and was pounding on the door, trying to wake the sheriff up, when Mr. Garble appeared with a pistol in his hand.

"Stop that racket!" Mr. Garble commanded

in a low voice. "Now turn around and walk right back out of the gate."

But he was too late, for as the burglar turned, the door opened and the sheriff stuck his head out. "Hey, you!" he exclaimed. "Come back here!" And then, as Mike faced around again: "Why, it's you, Mike! What in time—"

"Arrest that man, sheriff," Mr. Garble shouted, for it was now of course impossible to keep Mike from telling the sheriff his story.

"Arrest him!" the sheriff exclaimed. "I can't —he's already arrested; he's one of my prisoners."

"He was *my* prisoner just a few minutes ago," protested Mr. Garble. "Caught him breaking into my sister's house—him and that educated pig of Bean's. Burglary, that's what it was. And I want him arrested."

"Burglary, hey?" said the sheriff. "Well, that's Mike's business, burglary. What do you expect him to be doin'? Though I admit he ain't supposed to do any burgling when he's in jail."

"Look, sheriff," said Mike, "this Garble kidnapped a couple of Freddy's friends and locked 'em up in his cellar. They ain't anybody you or I would be real palsy with—just a couple of chickens—but I suppose some folks could get fond of 'em; anyway Freddy is, and I went with him to rescue 'em."

"Well, and where's Freddy?" the sheriff demanded. "Can't we get this over with? I want to go back to bed." He yawned. "Excuse me. See here, Garble, can't you come back after breakfast and we'll talk this over?"

"Freddy escaped too," said Mr. Garble quickly, for he didn't want the sheriff interfering with his plan to ship the pig off to Montana. "And all this talk about a rescue," he said, "is a lie. Look here—look at what's all over this man's shirt, sheriff. They broke in the house for just one purpose—to steal strawberry jam. Who were they rescuing in my sister's jam closet? What did opening quart jars of jam, and getting smeared all up with the stuff, have to do with any kind of rescue work?"

The sheriff frowned. "Why, Mike, that's a serious charge," he said. "That reflects on the kind of meals we been serving you here at the jail. Why, you've always had all the jam and pickles and stuff you wanted—even mustard pickles with your breakfast. Toast and jam between meals, too. Don't you *like* our jam? I make it all myself. And I always use only the best materials."

"Sure, I like it," said Mike. "I wasn't stealing jam at this guy's house. Like I told you, me and Freddy . . . Oh, gosh, sheriff, let me come in and change my shirt, will you? This sticky stuff all over my stomach makes me all goose flesh."

So the sheriff let him in, and after some more argument, Mr. Garble went home. "But you haven't heard the last of this," he said threateningly. "When my sister hears about the way you've—"

"G'night, Herbie," said the sheriff, and slammed the door in his face.

When Mike had changed his shirt, he told the sheriff his story. Of course he thought that Freddy had escaped too, because Mr. Garble had said so. The chickens would have to be rescued, but both Mike and the sheriff felt that the rescue could wait until after breakfast. But as it wouldn't be breakfast time for several hours, they both went to bed.

They got up again about the time when Mrs. Bean was steering the flying saucer up Salina Street in Syracuse. One of the Martians sat before a sort of box with buttons and dials on it, like a radio, and controlled the height and speed. Most of the time they stayed up high enough to keep clear of wires and things such as flagpoles that projected from the buildings, but for a few blocks they dropped down into the early morning traffic, and drove right along among the cars, about a foot above the pavement. People were going to work, and it was lots of fun to see them stop and drop their jaws and stare. Of course this was not surprising, for though many people in Syracuse had seen flying saucers in the night sky, very few had seen one driving up Salina Street through traffic, and even stopping for a red light.

"Good land, there's Amos Walnutt!" Mrs. Bean exclaimed. This was when they were coasting along about fifteen feet above the pavement. She called Click-two-squeaks's attention to Mr. Walnutt, who was her sister's husband's uncle, and the Martian brought the saucer down to hover just above and in front of the old gentleman. He looked up in alarm, saw Mrs. Bean and Mrs. Peppercorn waving to him from the window of the incredible vehicle, and forgetting all about the rheumatism which had made him lame for the last ten years, he gave a loud yell, dropped his cane, and sprinted off down the street.

"Well! . . . Gracious!" Mrs. Bean said. She looked rather put out. "What's he want to do that for? I haven't changed so much in the two years since I've seen him that he has to start screaming when he sees me unexpectedly."

"Didn't know you were keeping company with spiders, likely," Mr. Bean remarked.

He forgot all about the rheumatism which had made him
lame for the last ten years.

The Martians were making a sort of fizzing noise which Mr. Webb said was their laughter. "Sounds a good deal the way you do when you laugh, Mr. B.," Mrs. Bean said.

"There's said to be some spider blood in the Bean family, way back," said Mr. Bean, and began fizzing, as if to prove it.

"Spiders in the Bean family tree, eh?" said his wife. "I'm not surprised."

Click-two-squeaks had taken the saucer up again, for while they were motionless so close to the street, old Mr. Walnutt was not the only one who had panicked. At first, people had just stared, but when they realized what they were looking at, they ducked around corners and dived into doorways, and cars stopped and their occupants scrambled out and ran.

"Guess you better head back for Centerboro, Mrs. B.," said Mr. Bean. " 'Tain't seemly for you to be startin' a riot at your time of life. Anyway, I guess these spider-boys are anxious to see what those Martians of Herb Garble's look like."

When this was interpreted through the Webbs to the Martians, Click-two-squeaks patted Mr. Bean on the head with his feelers, which Mr. Webb said indicated that he appreciated his thoughtfulness. "He thinks Mrs. Bean

better let him steer now," said the spider, "because he's going to drive—my goodness, I think
he said a hundred miles a minute! Anyway, I
guess she wouldn't want to steer at that speed."

Mrs. Bean certainly didn't, and she was glad
to turn the tiller over to Click-two-squeaks. It
was a good thing she did. They covered the fifty-
odd miles from Syracuse to Centerboro in about
fifteen seconds.

The saucer landed in an open space behind
the big tent, unobserved by anybody but Mr.
Hercules, who was practicing juggling ten-
pound cannon balls. He just glanced at it.
"Guess 'Restes huz got one o' thum new sport
cars," he said, and went on juggling. Even
when the Martians trooped over to the side-
show tent, followed by the Beans, he paid no
special attention.

Although it was early, a line had already
formed before the tent containing Mr. Garble's
imitation Martians. It melted away quickly
when the real Martians approached. Even
though they were accompanied by four humans,
walking along hand in hand with them, very
few people seemed interested in getting a closer
look at them.

Mr. Garble was at the door, taking in the admission money. He turned pale when the

spider-men came up, holding out the half-dollars with which Mr. Bean had provided them. But though his teeth chattered, he took the money.

"These are real Martians, Mr. Garble," Mrs. Bean explained. "They seem to think that the ones you've been exhibiting aren't just what you claim they are."

"And let me tell you, young Herbert," added Mrs. Peppercorn, "if they ain't—well, just look at 'em. Four hands apiece they've got, and seven fingers on each hand. That's fine for playing duets with themselves on the piano, and it's also fine for tearing any party or parties they're kind of disappointed in into small pieces. Why, Herbert, where you goin'?" For the last they saw of Mr. Garble was his heels disappearing around the corner of the tent.

So the Martians filed in. The Horribles, disguised in the red suits, were sitting around the table, having a breakfast of lettuce leaves. When they saw the spider-men they jumped up and backed off into a corner, and Jinx arched his back and spat. But then they saw the Beans and Mrs. Peppercorn, and they relaxed and came forward. So when Mrs. Bean had explained about the Martians, Jinx explained about the Horribles. "It was Freddy's plan," he said, "to protect Mr. Boomschmidt from being called a faker. And by the way, where is Freddy?"

Nobody knew, though the first part of an answer was presently given them by the sheriff and Red Mike, who appeared in the tent door. They, too, were looking for Freddy. They were naturally much startled by the spider-men, but shook hands with them politely. "Boy, oh boy!" Mike exclaimed. "Four hands and twenty-eight fingers! What burglars I could make of 'em! Or pickpockets! Shake hands with a man with one hand, brush dust off his shoulder with another, and all the time be sliding his watch out of one pocket and his wallet out of another with the other two hands. D'you suppose, sheriff, after I got through here, I could maybe . . . But no, I guess it wouldn't do. All those fingers, though; what a waste!"

The Martians seemed very much amused by the attempt of Mr. Garble to imagine what real Martians must look like, and they fizzed with their queer laughter and insisted on going into the cage and trying out the chairs and beds and the various other furnishings. When Mr. Webb had told them the whole story, how Freddy had replaced the rats with his own friends, the rabbits, they laughed harder than ever, and shook hands with the Horribles and whacked them on the back and made a great fuss over them. So then the Horribles did their dance for them, and chanted:

"We are the Horrible Six.
We'll give you slaps, pinches, and kicks.
 We're mean and malicious,
 We're really quite vicious,
And if you complain of our tricks
We'll bust all your windows with bricks.
We'll watch; when we see that you've gone
To the movies, we'll dig up your lawn,
 We'll bite off the heads
 Of the flowers in your beds;
We'll get in the house and we'll soap all the treads
Of the stairs, and we'll tear all the carpets to shreds.
And when you come back from the show
We'll be up in the attic, and oh!
What queer noises you'll hear overhead
As soon as you get into bed!
You'll hear thumps on the floor, you'll hear squeaks in the wall;
Outside of your door in the dark upstairs hall
Something enormous will slither and crawl—
Your hair will stand up on your head!
 Beware! Do not mix

With the Horrible Six,
Or you'll be in a terrible fix!"

"Well," said the sheriff, "this is all very high-class entertainment, but Mike and me, we've got to go up to Mrs. Underdunk's and rescue those chickens."

When this had been explained to the Martians, they said they'd like to go along. But the sheriff was doubtful. "I dunno," he said. "I suppose I could swear 'em in as deputies. Although—"

A startled "Woof!" from the tent door made him turn, and there stood Leo, staring with amazement at the spider-men. "Well, file my toenails!" he exclaimed. "Golly, Uncle Ajax was telling me the truth about the goblins! Only time he ever did, I'll wager. But where are the caps with red tassels? Where'd you capture 'em, sheriff?"

The sheriff explained.

"You mean," said the lion, "that they're free to come *out* of that cage?" He shook his head doubtfully. "Well then, you'll excuse me if I just run along." He backed out.

But Jinx called after him. "Come back, Leo. These guys are friends. And we need your help."

From outside, Leo's voice replied: "You're going to need it worse before long or I miss my guess. So long, cat. I'll be seeing you. Or not, as the case may be." They heard the thump of his big paws as he trotted off.

The sheriff finally consented to let the Martians join the rescue party. The Horribles wanted to go too, but Jinx said they'd have to stay; they'd be letting Mr. Boomschmidt down if they left the Martian cage empty. So they got Bill Wonks to stand at the door and take admissions, and started off, taking Jinx and Mr. Hercules along with them. The Beans and Mrs. Peppercorn and Uncle Ben got back into the saucer, taking Squeak-squeak with them to drive them back to the farm and see if they could find Freddy.

It was just about this time that Mr. Garble was sitting at breakfast in the dining room of the Underdunk house. His sister was breakfasting upstairs in bed. It was a large gloomy room, and dozens of Underdunk ancestors stared down at Mr. Garble from the walls. Their stares—disapproving or ferocious or disgusted—always took away his appetite. But this morning he had no appetite anyway. He just sat and let his oatmeal get cold and glared back at them.

Then the chauffeur came in. He had his cap in his hand and his nose was swelled to about twice its normal size and he said. "If you're ready to go, sir, I think the Tushville express office will be open now."

So Mr. Garble got up, and they went down cellar. A large crate stood on the floor. It had three tags on it. One said: "Mr. Orville P. Garble, Twin Buttes, Montana." Another said: "Livestock. Rush. Water daily." The third said: "Fragile. Do not crush." And inside the crate was Freddy.

And they were just lifting the crate to carry it up the cellar stairs to the station wagon, when from somewhere in the upper part of the house came a long, terrible shriek.

They set the crate down again. And there came another even more terrible scream, which made the hair on the back of Mr. Garble's neck stand right up straight.

The chauffeur, however, didn't seem greatly disturbed. "Must be something wrong," he said. "Maybe you better go up and see."

Mr. Garble pulled his pistol from his pocket. "You're going, too," he said. "Ahead of me," he added.

Smith looked at the pistol. "Is that an order?" he asked.

"Go on," said Mr. Garble, poking the pistol at him. But Smith whirled suddenly, knocked the pistol from Mr. Garble's hand, and then dove for it. He was up in a second. And as a third and even more agonized screech rang through the house: "No," he said. "You're going. And alone."

Mr. Garble looked at the pistol and the pistol looked back at him with its one black eye. Then he went.

CHAPTER

16

The rescue party's plan of campaign had been organized by the sheriff. He and Mike would go right up on the front porch and pound on the door and demand admission. If it was refused, Mike had a hammer with which he would bang on the lock to snap it open. Mr. Hercules would guard the back door and capture anybody who tried to escape. The Martians and Jinx would remain concealed in the shrubbery about the house; they would seize any opportunity to get inside that presented itself.

But either the Martians didn't understand the plan, or their enthusiasm got the better of them, for before the sheriff and Mike were halfway up the front walk they made a rush for the house. They went up the side just like spiders, and popped in—one, two, three, four, five —an open window in the second story. And there was Mrs. Underdunk sitting up in bed with a breakfast tray on her lap, just taking the first sip of her morning coffee.

That was when she gave her first scream, and you can hardly blame her. Some people scream when they see just a small spider; but here were spider-men two feet high climbing in her bedroom window. So she screamed and her arm jerked up and the coffee cup flew up in the air and landed on the black dressing gown with gold dragons on it, and the tray went on the floor with a crash, and Mrs. Underdunk burrowed down under the bedclothes as far as she could go.

Now Martians are very mild and good tempered people, in spite of their odd appearance, and they wouldn't have hurt Mrs. Underdunk for worlds. But, as they told Mr. Webb afterwards, when she dove under the bedclothes, they thought her behavior strange. They didn't, of course, realize how frightening their appearance was to her, because it naturally wasn't in the least frightening to them. They thought maybe she was playing some childish game—peek-a-boo, perhaps. They had perched in a row on the foot of the bed. And Two-clicks said: "Well, if this silly creature wants to play, maybe we ought to play with her." So they jumped down on the bed and began pulling at the covers. And pretty soon they got her head out, and that was when she gave the second scream.

The bed had a very soft and springy mattress, and when the Martians jumped down on it, they bounced. This was something new to them, because of course they don't have much upholstered furniture on Mars. So they kept on jumping and bouncing around and squeaking with delight. To Mrs. Underdunk it probably seemed much the sort of dance that the Indians performed around the victim at the stake. So she let out her third and most terrible shriek, and burrowed down among the bedclothes again.

Two-squeaks said: "This seems to me rather a silly game. It's all very well to be pleasant to these earth-people, but for goodness' sake let's act a little more grown-up. Let's go downstairs and see how the rescue is getting on." So they jumped off the bed and went out into the hall and started down the stairs. And met Mr. Garble coming up.

Mr. Garble was a very dishonest man, but he was not especially cowardly. It is easy to criticize his behavior at this point, but it seems hardly fair. For to start up the stairs in your own house and meet five spider-men coming down is enough to unhinge anybody. Mr. Garble gave a shriek which was louder than all three of his sister's put together. He made one jump to the foot of the stairs. The front door, he knew, was unlocked, and he started for it, but just as he took hold of the knob he saw the figures of Mike and the sheriff through the glass. He turned and dashed through hall and kitchen to the back door.

Mr. Hercules hadn't understood his instructions very well either. He saw no point in waiting outside to grab anybody that might come out. Much better, he thought, to go in and get them. The back door was locked, so he just put one big hand against it and shoved. There was a ripping sound as lock and hinges gave way, and the door fell inward with a bang.

And there was Mr. Garble, sprinting along the hall towards it.

It didn't occur to Mr. Hercules that Mr. Garble, whom he knew, was a person who should be stopped. "Hullo, Muster Garble," he said. "Coming out?" And stood politely aside. And Mr. Garble, who was no fool, said: "Thank you, Herc," and sprinted right on past the conservatory and the garage and hurdled the hedge and vanished.

At the front door, after his ringing and pounding got no answer, Mike took his hammer and struck a sharp blow just above the lock. Then he turned the knob and opened the door. "See how easy 'tis?" he said proudly. "Just one tap and she flies open. But you have to know just where to hit her." The sheriff, who knew that the door hadn't been locked at all, and indeed was even slightly ajar, said nothing, for he didn't want to hurt Mike's feelings. A minute later they were down cellar knocking the slats off Freddy's crate.

As soon as Freddy was free, the three released Mrs. Hapgood and the two chickens, and then went upstairs to the back door, where a lot of squeaking was going on. They found Mr. Hercules entertaining the Martians by tossing them in the air and catching them again. They curled up their arms and legs just as a spider does, so that they were like black balls, and then he began juggling three at a time. They squeaked with delight.

"Seen Garble, Herc?" the sheriff asked.

"Ol' Moosiludge, huh?" said Mr. Hercules. "Yuh, he come out. Chasin' somebody, Uh guess. Went off in thut direction." He pointed.

"Oh, for Pete's sake!" said the sheriff. "Why didn't you stop him? That's what we told you to do."

"Stop ol' Moosiludge Garble?" Mr. Hercules was puzzled. "Yuh didn't say nothin' about stopping him. Stop anybody, yuh said. He ain't anybody, he's ol' Moosiludge." He began to laugh. "Moosiludge!" he said. "Uh, uh, uh!"

While this was going on, Freddy was trying to calm Mrs. Hapgood and Little Broiler, who were frightened by the appearance of the Martians. Chiquita was not scared; she even asked Mr. Hercules to throw her up in the air, too. But Mrs. Hapgood fluttered and clucked and gave little squawks of alarm, and she got Broiler to follow her into a hidden place under a hedge, where she tucked the weeping little creature out of sight under her wing.

Freddy stood by the hedge and said: "These people won't hurt you, madam. They came to rescue you."

But Mrs. Hapgood just kept giving her hysterical yelps. "Oh! Oh! Oh, Broiler, be very still; perhaps they won't see us."

"They can hear you a mile off," said Jinx, coming up. "If they'd wanted to eat you, you'd be nothing but a couple of claws and a few feathers floating down the wind by this time. Come on, Broiler, come out here—we want to take you home."

"He can't hear you," said Chiquita. "He's under her wing. She was always trying to get us under her wings. I kept telling her that we were too old for that silly kid stuff, but you can't tell her anything."

The sheriff came over to them. "Is that the hen that can whistle 'Dixie'?" he asked. And when Freddy said it was, he said: "I understand Garble paid quite a lot of money for her. Like to see her."

"Your wish is my command," said Jinx with a grin, and he dived under the hedge where there was a lot of squawking for a minute, and then he came out dragging Mrs. Hapgood by her tailfeathers. Little Broiler followed, peeping miserably.

The sheriff took the hen up and looked at her. "Not much to look at," he said. "Eh, Mike?"

"You wouldn't dare say such a thing if the

He came out dragging Mrs. Hapgood by her tailfeathers.

late Mr. Hapgood was alive," said the hen huffily. "He'd peck your eyes out."

"Just as well he's not still with us, then," said the sheriff. "Well, ma'am, what are we going to do with you? We'll take these two chickens back home, but how about you? You're Garble's property in the eyes of the law, and as I'm the law here in Centerboro, I can't very well take you away from him."

"My childhood home is Hubbersburg, West Virginia, but I do not wish to return there," said the hen, who had become somewhat calmer. "My talents were never appreciated there. Mr. Garble, however, believed that there was a great future before me if I could appear on a wider stage than that of our local Odd Fellows' Hall. He has promised me a star part in his circus."

"It ain't a very big circus," Jinx remarked.

"It will be," said Mrs. Hapgood confidently, "as soon as the public get acquainted with my repertoire."

The sheriff spoke behind his hand to Freddy. "What's that?"

"Your repertoire is all the tunes you can play," said the pig. "Right now I guess it's just 'Dixie.' "

"Kind of like a bill of fare with just pickled onions on it," said the sheriff.

Mrs. Hapgood had of course heard this.

" 'Dixie' is just the beginning. I have already begun practicing others. I am now working on 'Pop Goes the Weasel.' A very difficult composition, requiring a high degree of skill. If you would care to—"

"Thank you," said Freddy hastily, "I'm afraid we haven't time. We must first decide what is to be done with you. You don't want to go back to your home—"

"No. It will perhaps be better if I stay here. I am not accustomed to being confined in a cellar. The damp is bad for my voice, and there is very little social life. Yet I have every confidence that the excellent Garble, though he knows little about music himself, will give me my chance. He—"

"Just a minute," Jinx interrupted, and drew Freddy aside. "If I'm not mistaken," he said, "the excellent Garble is up in that big pine tree over in the other block, watching us. If we want to capture him—"

"I don't, specially," Freddy said. "Not publicly. But I've got an idea. The lot of us had better go back to the circus grounds. Let him see us go, and take that musical hen with us. Then we can circle back. Come here a minute, you and Mike, sheriff. "Listen." He outlined his plan.

The sheriff shook his head. " 'Tain't legal."

"Oh, phooey!" said Jinx. "It's fun, isn't it? And justice, too. Well, go on back to your old jail and be legal, then. If you don't see it happen, you won't know anything about it."

"Oh, come on, sheriff," Mike said. "Suppose it ain't legal; you can arrest yourself afterwards, can't you, and put yourself in jail? If you want to be real strict about it, you can lock yourself in."

"Well," said the sheriff, who didn't want to miss the fun, "if you put it that way . . . Hey, Herc! Come on. Stick those chickens in your pocket. I'll carry this Mrs. What's-your-name."

"Hapgood," snapped the hen. "Mrs. C. Ogden Hapgood. Madame Gloriana Hapgood, on the stage."

"Excuse me, ma'am," said the sheriff.

"Don't mention it, I'm sure," the hen replied graciously.

CHAPTER

17

As they marched off down the street they could still see Mr. Garble perched in the pine tree, watching them. As soon as they were gone, Freddy felt sure that he would return to the house to get the pistol he had dropped; and probably he had enough affection for his sister to make sure that the Martians hadn't done her any harm. What would he do then? Well, he would want to recover the talented hen. And he would want to take revenge on Freddy. Most likely he would go out to the Grimby house and get the rats. He might even openly attack the farm.

The first part of Freddy's plan, therefore, was to ambush Mr. Garble and capture him. The simplest way to do this would be to lie in wait inside the house, but it wouldn't be easy for them to get into the house, if he was watching. So when they had gone several blocks he sent Mr. Hercules on to the circus with Mrs. Hapgood and the two chickens, and the rest of the party doubled back through gardens and behind hedges and hid themselves in a big clump of shrubbery which divided the Underdunk garden from the front lawn. One of the Martians climbed a tree and kept watch.

After five minutes or so the sentinel began click-squeaking at a great rate, and Mr. Webb, who was on Freddy's ear, said: "It's Garble. He's creeping up through that back yard next door." So Freddy nodded to the sheriff, who pursed up his lips and whistled the first bars of "Dixie."

Nothing happened for a minute, then a head popped up over the hedge at one side of the lawn. And the sheriff whistled: *"I wish I was in Dixie. Away! Away!"*

Mr. Garble pushed through the hedge and ran, crouching low, towards the bushes. "Here chick!" he called. "Here chick, chick, chick!"

Mike and the sheriff were hanging onto each other, for they had both been overcome by a fit of the giggles. Freddy glowered at them and shook his head. The sheriff, with both hands over his mouth, nodded, and then managed to control himself. Mike did, too. He wiped the grin off his face and turned his back for a minute. And then, as Mr. Garble crept closer to the bush, the burglar imitated a cackling hen. "A-a-awk, quk-wuk-wuk-wuk!"

It was a pretty good imitation, but it didn't quite fool Mr. Garble. He stopped short, a look of suspicion came over his face, and he started to back cautiously away. Freddy was sure that in a second or two he would whirl and make a break. They would never catch him again.

"Stop him!" Freddy shouted, and dashed out.

Mr. Garble turned and ran. But Freddy was a skilled football player, and he was fast. He caught up with the man, then when he was even with him, swerved and threw his shoulder into him and knocked him off his feet. Before Garble could get up, Mike and the sheriff and the Martians were on him. They led him into the house, and down into the cellar, and they shoved him into the crate and nailed it fast.

"Well, Mike," said Freddy, "you pretty near wrecked us. I wish you'd stick to burgling and not try animal imitations." He looked with satisfaction at the crate. "It's got the labels on it and everything," he said. "All we've got to do is get him to the express office. Wonder where Uncle Ben is."

"You can't ship him express," said the sheriff. "I mean, you can ship him, all right, but will he stay shipped? Some busybody will let him out."

"You're darn right he will," said Mr. Garble. "See here, pig: you let me out of here and we'll call it square. I won't make any complaint against you. But you'll get yourself in a peck of trouble sending me to Montana. Even if I got there, I'd just come right back."

"Sure," said Freddy. "But we think it would be kind of fun to give you the trip. Still, come to think of it, it's no kind of revenge for me. You were going to have me sent out there to be turned into chops and bacon. Well, I can do that right here. I'll just turn you over to these Martians; they'll have a real feast tonight."

Mr. Webb had taken refuge in Freddy's ear when the pig started after Mr. Garble. Now he said: "My goodness, Freddy, the Martians would be horrified if I told 'em what you just said. They aren't savages. They just eat cereals and stuff."

"Sure, I know that," Freddy said. "Come out of my ear, Webb; you tickle."

Mr. Garble had begun to yell for help at the top of his lungs. Under cover of the noise, Freddy said to Mr. Webb: "I want to scare him, make him think he's going to be eaten. Good gracious, Webb, don't you know what he and his rats are trying to do? They want to drive the Beans away from the farm—want to get it for themselves. So look, get the Martians to play up—you know, pretend they're fattening him up like the witch did Hansel and Gretel. If we give him a good scare, maybe we can keep him from trying anything against the Beans. Then we'll let him go."

The sheriff was worried. If someone heard the yells for help, and came in and found him aiding and abetting a kidnapping, he might lose his job as sheriff. So he dragged an old carpet out of a corner and pulled it over the crate. Now the muffled yells that came from under it couldn't be heard even up in the kitchen.

Mr. Webb hopped over to Two-clicks's shoulder. In a minute there was a lot of clicking and squeaking and fizzing Martian laughter, and then the carpet was pulled off the crate and several seven-fingered hands reached in and felt of Mr. Garble's arms and legs.

"They think you aren't quite fat enough yet, Mr. Garble," Freddy said.

Mr. Webb had come back to Freddy's shoulder. "They say they'll deliver Garble in Montana for you, if you want them to. Funny thing, they seem to know that Hansel and Gretel story, and they say why not let him think they're taking him to Mars to be fattened up for the stew pot?"

Freddy began to be a little sorry for Mr. Garble. But he remembered all the attempts that Garble had made on his life, and he decided that a good scare would do such a cruel and dishonest person no harm. It might at least make him think twice before he started to cause the Beans any trouble. So he said: "All right. But their saucer's over at the circus grounds. We'll have to send one of them for it, but if they start walking through the street, they'll be mobbed."

"Garble's car is out in the garage," said the sheriff. "I'll drive one of 'em over." So he did, and when the saucer had been brought down in the Underdunk driveway, and the sheriff had returned, he and Mike and the Martians hauled the crate upstairs and hoisted it into the saucer.

Mr. Garble was by this time so hoarse from yelling for help that he could hardly speak above a whisper, so none of the neighbors noticed that anything unusual was going on. Jinx, who had decided to go along for the ride, hopped in, the hatch was closed, the saucer began to whirl slowly, then with a whoosh! like a giant rocket, shot up and vanished almost instantly in the western sky.

"I hope we haven't made a mistake," Freddy said. "But Webb says they'll be back here in an hour or less."

"From Montana?" said the sheriff. "You're crazy!"

"I wouldn't be surprised if I was," said the pig. "But there wasn't much of anything else we could do. They'll deliver him to his uncle's ranch, and I suppose his uncle will pay his fare back to Centerboro. But he won't be anxious to try to get even with us." He sighed. "Oh, well, while we're waiting I think I'd better run up and see that Mrs. Underdunk is all right."

"You might better run up and jump off the roof," said the sheriff. "My guess is she ain't feelin' real sociable right now. And Garble's pistol is in the house. She probably ain't a very good shot, but if you'll excuse me sayin' so, you're a pretty sizable target . . . Oh, well, if you insist on it, I'll go up with you."

Mrs. Underdunk was nowhere on the ground floor. They scouted cautiously. The pistol wasn't where Mr. Garble had dropped it. This was not reassuring, and the sheriff urged Freddy to get out while he was still un-punctured. But, though Freddy realized that Mrs. Underdunk would be only too happy to shoot him, he remembered those screams. Any-body that screamed like that was pretty scared, and he had a lot of sympathy with scared peo-ple. He had often been badly scared himself, and he knew what it was like. So he crept up the front stairs, followed at a safe distance by the reluctant sheriff.

The door to the large room at the head of the stairs was closed. He tapped lightly on it, then stood to one side. The sheriff dropped on the stairs; his eyes came just above the top step. "Mrs. Underdunk?" Freddy called. "Are you all right?"

"Who is there?" quavered Mrs. Underdunk's voice.

"It's me, Freddy," said the pig. "I just wanted to—"

Bang! went the big pistol, and splinters flew outward from the middle of the door.

"She's all right," said the sheriff. He didn't get up, but slithered backwards down the stairs on his stomach. He made remarkable speed, but

*BANG! went the big pistol, and splinters flew outside
from the middle of the door.*

Freddy was ahead of him at the bottom step.

"Yeah," said the pig. "She seems to be."

It was a little over an hour later that the saucer returned. Jinx hopped out.

"Boy, what an experience!" he said.

"Did you really go to Montana?" Mike asked, and Freddy said: "What was it like?"

"Yeah, we went there all right," said the cat. "Delivered our livestock at the Twin Buttes railroad station. Like?" he said. "Gosh, I don't know what it was like. Spider-boy, he just sat there and twisted dials and things for half an hour, and we were there. Same coming back. Boy, *what* an experience!"

"Yeah," said the sheriff dryly. "Must have been. Like sitting in the dentist's waiting room, only with no old magazines."

"Did you see when you crossed the Mississippi?" Freddy asked.

"How could I at that speed?" Jinx said. "Everything was just a blur."

"Sure must have been stimulating," Mike remarked.

"But what an *experience!*" Jinx repeated. That was all they could get out of him. Still, there are lots of people who travel all over Europe and haven't much more to say about it.

So then they all got into the saucer and went back to the circus grounds.

CHAPTER

18

The Horribles were still in their cage, and people were filing through and looking at them at fifty cents a head. Mr. Hercules had taken the Beans and Uncle Ben home, but Bill Wonks had had to go help Mr. Boomschmidt get things ready for the big show, and Mrs.

Peppercorn had agreed to stay for a while and take in the fifty-cent pieces.

"Well, sheriff," she said as they came up, "I hope you've got young Herbert locked up and out of harm's way."

"He's out of harm's way all right," said the sheriff. "Takin' a little trip for his health."

"Hope it's a long one," she replied.

> *"Not that I have ever felt*
> *Very much interest in Garble's healt'."*

The sheriff said: "Yeah," in a tired voice, and Freddy said: "I'm glad you're here, Mrs. Peppercorn, instead of anybody else. The Martians have agreed to take the place of the Horribles for a while, and we want to sneak 'em in and sneak the Horribles out without telling Mr. Boom. Because if he knows he's been showing fake Martians, he's so darned honest that he'll tell everybody, and apologize in the newspapers, and I don't know what all. It might very well ruin his reputation. We've got to protect him. So we'll tell him, and we'll tell the people that visit the show, that now that warm weather has come, the Martians have taken off their red suits."

"And shaved off those red whiskers," put in Jinx.

Freddy said: "Yes."

"And cut off their long noses," said Mike.

"Well," said Freddy, "the rabbits had shorter noses than the rats, and nobody noticed. I bet nobody says a word. Because mostly these people that come haven't been here before."

So they had the rabbits take off the red suits and hang them up on the pegs with the nightshirts, and then sneaked them out and the real Martians in. And as Freddy had guessed, nobody noticed the difference. Only one woman said anything. She had been in before, and she said: "I don't remember that they was so dark complected. And I guess I missed that third eye the time I saw 'em before." But she didn't complain.

When everything seemed to be going smoothly, Freddy got Two-clicks to drive him and the Horribles back to the farm in the saucer. Jinx wasn't going to go at first, but then he decided to. "I like this here vehicle, darned if I don't," he said. "Think I'll get me one when the new models come out. Home, James," he said to Two-clicks as he climbed in.

There was bad news at the farm. Simon had escaped from the parrot cage; he had managed to break or gnaw two of the wires and then bend them apart so that he could slip through. And in the early morning hours—presumably under Simon's leadership—the rats had come down from the Grimby house and raided Mr. Bean's vegetable garden. It was pure vandalism; none of the vegetables were ready to eat yet, except a few radishes. They had cut all the plants off close to the ground.

A year or so earlier the animals had formed the First Animal Republic, and had elected Mrs. Wiggins President. They had raised an army and had fought a serious and successful campaign against the rats, who had had their headquarters in that same Grimby house, deserted then, but still standing, where they now again had taken up residence. After this the F.A.R. had demobilized its army, keeping only a small standing honor-guard of rabbits to handle emergencies, and to guard the President when she made her annual speech on May 3rd, the date on which the F.A.R. had been founded. The official flag was raised only on this date, and on a few special holidays.

To this rule there was one exception. When a national emergency arose and it was desired to call a full meeting of all the citizens, the flag was raised over the barn. This could only be done by executive order—that is, by the command of Mrs. Wiggins. And there was a good deal of ceremony about it. It wasn't enough just to tell Mrs. Wiggins that a national emergency existed; Freddy had to write it all out in proper form and send it by messenger. Then the honor-guard had to assemble and stand at attention while the flag was being raised. And Mrs. Wiggins made a formal speech.

Some animals felt that all this ceremony was just a waste of time. They called it red tape, and said it was nonsense. But Mrs. Wiggins, though not brilliant, had great common sense, and she knew that her presidential orders had to be issued with a whole lot of ceremony. Otherwise the animals would say: "Oh, it's just Mrs. Wiggins. We don't have to do what *she* says."

So the flag went up. And within half an hour every animal and bird on the farm knew about it. For those who had seen the flag told those who had not, and at half past seven that evening they began streaming towards the barn, which was soon packed to the doors. It would take too long to list the distinguished members of that gathering. Besides all the animals who lived around the barnyard, there were among those present Old Whibley and his niece, Vera, the owls; Uncle Solomon, the screech owl; Peter, the bear; and Mac, the wildcat, from the Big Woods; Theodore, the frog; a lot of backwoods characters from outlying burrows; and several small delegations from neighbor-

ing farms. Birds sat wing to wing on every
rafter, and there were hundreds of small animals—mice and rabbits and squirrels and
skunks—even Cecil, the porcupine, came. But
of course Cecil liked to go to meetings, because
the other animals always gave him plenty of
room. And Leo was there; Two-clicks had
flown him up to the farm in the saucer.

The meeting opened as usual with the singing of the animals' marching song. The words
of this are today so familiar to every school child
that they are not set down here. Then, since
there was plenty of time, Charles was called
upon to open the proceedings with a speech.

Charles's speeches were so magnificent and
noble sounding, he used so many long and
high-flown words, that very few animals could
listen to one of them without becoming wildly
enthusiastic. Just what they were enthusiastic
about they were never quite certain, since, when
you thought about the speech afterwards, you
were never sure what it meant. But the animals
always enjoyed them, and they were indeed
very useful, for when Charles sat down—
or was pulled down, as sometimes happened—
Freddy or Mrs. Wiggins would tell what action
was proposed, and the enthusiasm was right
there to carry it through. This is the real purpose of most speeches.

"Ladies and gentlemen," Charles began. "You have been called together tonight, under the glorious banner of the F.A.R., because a grave crisis exists, a crisis which menaces not only our very existence as a nation of freeborn animals, birds, and bugs, but the entire future of the great Bean farm, and its noble owners, Mr. and Mrs. Bean.

"Pledged as we are to maintain and defend this great republic of ours; obligated by every tie of duty, affection, and gratitude to build with our bodies a living shield between that ancient stronghold of the Beans and the advance of a cruel and determined enemy, we must rise, my friends—I call upon you to rise in your might and smite that enemy hip and thigh, squash that enemy to a grease spot."

At this point there was prolonged cheering. When it had finally died down, Charles lowered his voice to a conversational tone. "We are indeed fortunate," he went on, "to have with us tonight representatives of two of the most powerful groups in—and I think I may say this without fear of contradiction—in the whole solar system. The first of these is our old friend, Leo, king of the beasts, and our ally on many a hard-fought field, representing Boomschmidt's Stupendous and Unexcelled Circus."

At this Leo rose and bowed selfconsciously.

"The other," Charles went on, "is a new friend, not known yet to many of you, although one to whom I, as a father, bear an overwhelming debt of gratitude. For it was he and his comrades who at risk of life and limb assisted in the gallant and daring rescue of my two dear children from the evil house of Underdunk. My wife Henrietta and myself owe to this new friend, for the return of our two precious darlings, far, far more than we can ever repay. I refer to the ambassador from Mars, the Honorable Two-clicks."

Mrs. Webb, who was sitting on the Martian's shoulder, translated this, and Two-clicks rose and waved his feelers in a gracious gesture of acknowledgment.

There was a great deal of applause, and Charles, wiping a tear from his eye with a small handkerchief which he produced from under his wing—he had brought it especially for this purpose—went on. "We of the F.A.R., therefore, will have as allies, if it comes to war—and I am afraid it will—we will have as allies not only ferocious and relentless lions and tigers, implacable rhinoceroses and hippopotamuses, savage hyenas and fierce and bellicose elephants, but Martians, too, will be our brothers in arms. Think of it, my friends: our ally will be the planet Mars! Why the very stars in their courses will be fighting for us!"

"Who we going to fight—the dictionary?" said a harsh voice, and Charles looked up to the rafter from which Old Whibley was staring down at him with fierce yellow eyes.

Charles glared back at him. "The voice which you just heard, my friends," he said, "is that of my aged and sagacious colleague, old hooter Whibley. As usual, he is attempting with sarcastic remarks to stir up trouble and dissension in a meeting which has but one purpose: to consider means of repulsing the attacks of a vicious enemy."

"Who?" said Whibley. "Whoo?"

Charles began to get mad. "What's the idea, sitting up there and hooting? Go on back to the woods, if you—"

"Who?" the owl interrupted. "I'm asking *who* we've got to fight! You go on ranting about an enemy, and you still don't tell us who the enemy is. When is that to be revealed—in the next installment?"

Charles lost his temper. "If you'll shut up and let me talk, I'll tell you! The rats! That's who the enemy is. Heavily entrenched on our very borders, they have already raided deep into our territory. Are we to sit here idle, with folded claws—or paws, as the case may be—"

"Don't forget hoofs," put in Whibley, and Uncle Solomon gave a peal of his tittering, derisive laughter. "Perhaps," said the screech owl, "you could somewhat abbreviate your remarks by using a collective noun—say, for example, 'with folded extremities.' " And he tittered again.

"Oh, shut up, both of you!" When Charles got really mad his speeches went all to pieces. "You owls make me sick, you're always so—"

"Perhaps I had better explain," Mrs. Wiggins interrupted. "As Charles says, it's those rats again, Simon and his gang." And she quickly outlined the situation. "And now," she said, "I want to remind you that once, several years ago, the rats held this very house, and we attacked it and defeated them. But at that time the house was standing. Today only the cellar is left; the rats have certainly dug themselves in, and an attack would merely drive them into their holes—holes so narrow that it would be impossible to pursue and capture them. So has anybody a plan?"

Charles was smarting from the treatment which the owls had given him. He hopped up on the dashboard of the old phaeton, and shouted: "Yes! I have a plan, and it is the only plan worthy of the glorious F.A.R. What! Shall we allow a mob of cheap gangster rats to defy the authority of our powerful state? We were not always so fearful. Not in the old days would we have stood aside, hat in hand, and let these robbers plunder and destroy our broad lands. No! Better to languish in chains in the dungeons of the Grimby house; better, I say, to lie stricken on a well-fought field, than to cringe and basely surrender to an enemy whom we have twice before defeated in battle. I call for an immediate attack on the Grimby cellar! I call for an immediate vote! And I publicly brand those who vote for appeasement as cowards and dastards!"

Freddy looked at Mrs. Wiggins. "The old fool!" he said angrily, as the animals began cheering wildly. "Now he's done it! All the birds and mice and rabbits that know they can't get in the fight anyway will vote for the attack."

And indeed that was what happened. "Pah!" said Old Whibley disgustedly. "Come along, Vera. Coming, Sol?" And the three owls floated silently out into the night.

Matters brought up before the general meeting of the F.A.R. were always decided by vote. Usually the wiser and more sober animals were able to discuss such matters, and see that no rash decisions were taken. But when they were taken, there was nothing those who had opposed them could do. Charles had forced the

"Yes, I have a plan."

issue. And his success had so gone to his head that he was now shouting: "If our appointed leaders hang back, my friends, I myself will lead you! Yes, with this beak and these claws I will smite the foemen. You know me, my friends; you know that I will not fail you. You know the story of that great duel at the bridge on the back road. Follow me, my friends, and where you see my tailfeathers floating above the fight, follow me on to victory."

He would have gone on, but Henrietta, irritated by a repetition of his bragging reference to the fight with the rat, jumped up beside him and cuffed him so soundly with her wings that he fell off the dashboard. "You noisy old rattle-beak!" she exclaimed. "Now shut up and let somebody with some sense talk, or your tailfeathers will float above the fight all right, but they won't be attached to you. You silly braggart!"

So then Freddy got up, and when he had managed to quiet the audience down somewhat, was able to persuade them that the attack on the cellar would have to be put off for three days. In that time, he hoped, they might be able to do something that would make the battle unnecessary.

CHAPTER
19

The next day Mr. Garble came back to Centerboro. His uncle had paid for his ticket home by
plane. He got over to the circus grounds as
soon as possible, and found Mrs. Peppercorn
taking in the half-dollars at the Martian tent.
She had become very much attached to the
Martians, and liked being with them so well
that she had agreed to stay on until they left.
Mr. Garble didn't like the arrangement, but

he liked being with real Martians even less, and
he went so far as to offer her a cent on every
dollar she took in. But she refused it. "I like
being with 'em," she said.

"Well, I don't," he said. "But as long as
they're making money for me . . . How long
are they going to stay?"

"You better ask them," said the old lady.

"I don't want to go near 'em," he said, and
shuddered. "How you can like them! . . ."

"A long time you have to be around of 'em,
    [she said],
Before you get really found of 'em."

A shadow fell across the tent door, and a
heavy voice said: "Uh, uh! If 'tain't ol'
Moosiludge! Uh, uh."

"Oh, gosh!" said Mr. Garble hopelessly.
"You still harping on that?"

"Yuh," said Mr. Hercules, " 's funny."

And then Mr. Garble had an inspiration. It
was about the only good idea he had ever had,
and it seems almost too bad that it turned
against him in the end. He said: "Look, Herc,
I heard one yesterday—golly, this will kill
you!" He began to laugh, and Mr. Hercules
looked happily expectant. "Listen, Herc. There
were these two Irishmen, Pat and Mike. Mike

said: 'Begorra, Pat, 'tis a foine day.' And Pat said—" He broke off, to roar with laughter. "Golly, I can't—can't—oh, ho, ho, *haw!*"

"Yuh, wha'd he say, Muster Garble?" Mr. Hercules asked, grinning broadly.

Mr. Garble mastered his mirth. "He said: 'So 'tis, Moike. So 'tis, if it don't rain.' " And then Mr. Garble broke down completely and slapped his thigh and shouted and sobbed. "Herc, Herc," he gasped, "isn't that a wonder —isn't that a dandy?"

Mr. Hercules's face broke into a sympathetic smile. He even managed to laugh slightly. "Uh, uh!" Then he stopped, looking puzzled. "Yuh," he said doubtfully, "but . . . yuh, 'if it don't rain.' Uh, uh, 's funny, Uh guess. Only . . . wull, 'if it don't rain'—Uh don't quite see . . ."

Mr. Garble was still doubled up, trying to control his merriment. "Think it over, Herc. You'll get it. And when you do—oh, boy!" And he went off, waving his arms and shouting: "Haw, haw, *haw!*" till the line of people waiting to see the Martians stared after him in amazement. Mr. Hercules, too, stared, then with a puzzled shake of his head went off to think it over.

Mr. Garble got in his car and drove to Dixon's diner and had a couple of hamburgers

with lots of onion, and a cup of coffee, and
then he drove around to the Big Woods by the
back road to see Simon. Within two minutes his
presence there was reported to Freddy by Mr.
J. J. Pomeroy, a robin who was one of the
sentinels posted along the edge of the woods
to keep an eye on the rats. Mr. Pomeroy was
head of the A.B.I., the Animal Bureau of In-
vestigation, and had under him a large corps
of birds, small animals, and bumblebees. The
information had been brought to him by a
bumblebee named Hector.

Bumble bees make excellent spies. They go
blundering along, bumping into things and
buzzing importantly, apparently absorbed in
their own rather stupid business. Nobody pays
much attention to them. But they have sharp
eyes and are good listeners. Nobody fools a
bumblebee, not for a minute. Having reported,
Hector returned at once to the enemy stronghold. He banged around close to a wide crack
in the cellar foundation, apparently interested
in a clump of dandelions. Several of the rats
saw him, as did Mr. Garble, but neither rats
nor Garbles know much about nature, or they
would have known that no bumblebee would
touch a dandelion with a ten-foot pole. Hector
heard the entire conversation between Simon
and Mr. Garble.

It was an angry conversation and they did a good deal of yelling; for Mr. Garble was mad because the rats had let themselves be kidnapped and replaced by real Martians, and Simon was mad because he didn't know where Zeke and Banjo and the three other rats had gone to. Of course neither of them knew about Freddy's scheme to substitute Horribles for rats, not that the four missing rats were still shut up in a rat-trap in Willy's cage. And of course each accused the other of knowing all about what had happened, and of lying about it.

"Well, you're no use to me any more," Mr. Garble said. "If you'd stayed where you agreed to, we could have made a lot of money together. As it is, these Martians will probably go back home in a few days, and the fun will be over. I gave you the Big Woods, and this house, and you can have it for all of me—though I don't think your title to it will stand up in the law courts."

"It had better stand up," Simon retorted. "Try to get it back and the story of a lot of your business deals will be published in the *Bean Home News.*"

"Pooh!" said Mr. Garble. "An animals' newspaper!"

Simon and the other rats backed away from him. "When you say 'Pooh' like that, move

"Well, you're no use to me any more!" Mr. Garble said.

back, will you? You've been eating onions," Simon said. "We don't like onions. We may be rats, but we have to draw the line somewhere."

Mr. Garble laughed. "You don't draw it at thievery, but you do at onions! That's a laugh. Well, I've told you you can have this place, I don't want it. But don't threaten me with that barnyard sheet."

"It was not a threat, it was a promise," said Simon. "And remember, what is in the *Bean Home News* one afternoon is in the *New York Times* next morning. So I suggest that you make a strong effort to find Zeke and Banjo and the rest of them."

"Sure, sure," said Mr. Garble. "I'll make a strong effort." He blew in Simon's face and then laughed. "Is that strong enough for you?"

Hector reported this to Mr. Pomeroy, who at once reported to Freddy. Freddy and Jinx and Mrs. Wiggins and Leo, who had come out to the farm to represent the circus in the council of war, had a long talk. And the result of it was that Freddy got Mr. Bean's permission and hitched up Hank to the phaeton and drove into Centerboro, where he stopped at the grocery store of Mr. Henry Molecule, and asked about the price of onions.

"Well, sir," said Mr. Molecule, "I got a few

here in the store, but they ain't very good. The new ones aren't in yet."

"I don't care about new ones," said Freddy. "Any old onions will do."

Mr. Molecule laughed. "I got plenty of old ones, all right. Ten bags that are going bad on me. But I'm afraid I haven't got any you'd want."

"I'll take the ten bags," said Freddy, and Mr. Molecule stared, and said: "Well, you can have 'em for nothing—save me drawing them to the dump."

So Freddy and Mr. Molecule and Mr. Molecule's helper put clothespins on their noses and loaded the onions into the phaeton, and Freddy drove out of Centerboro and up the back road between the Bean Woods and the Big Woods. There he unloaded the onions beside the bridge, covered them with a lot of old sacks, and came home. And he smelled so, just from being near the onions, that Mrs. Wiggins made him stand outside the doorway while he talked.

In his absence another report had come in. Hector had learned from a couple of young centipedes, who had just set up housekeeping under the second cellar step, that the rats planned another raid for that night. A meadow on the west side of the farm was planted to corn, which was now about six inches high, and they were going to pull it up.

"That'll be fine," Freddy said. "But now we've got to get some volunteers to cut up those onions. They'll smell twice as bad when they're chopped up."

"Oh no they won't," Mrs. Wiggins said. "Because if what I smell now with you standing there outside the door is any sort of faint suggestion of what they're like now, you won't scare up a single volunteer to even go and look at 'em."

"Sure is pretty rich," said Jinx. "But how about Sniffy and his family? They aren't what you'd call exactly sensitive to odors."

Sniffy Wilson and his wife Aroma were the parents of a large family of skunks who had been on the farm many years.

"Get hold of 'em, will you, Jinx?" Freddy said. "I want to go see Whibley. If Simon leads that raid tonight, and I'm pretty sure he will, maybe Whibley could capture him. When he escaped we lost the only thing we had to bargain with. We ought to get him back if we can."

Uncle Solomon was calling on Old Whibley when Freddy stopped by the tree in which the owl had his nest and tapped on the trunk.

The two owls were sitting on a high branch close to the nest. Neither of them appeared to have noticed Freddy's presence, but Whibley said: "Do you—ah—notice anything, Sol?"

The screech owl lifted his beak and sniffed. "H'm," he said. "Now that you mention it, yes. There is obviously something rotten in the state of Denmark."

"That's from Shakespeare," said Freddy.

"Dear me," said Uncle Solomon, looking down at the pig for the first time. "This smelly person appears to have the rudiments of culture. And from which play was the quotation, odoriferous one?"

"It's from *Hamlet,*" said Freddy. The Complete-Works-of-Shakespeare-in-One-Volume was one of his most prized possessions, although it had been used for a long time to prop up the broken leg of his bed.

Old Whibley's enormous yellow eyes looked down at him now for the first time. "And did you perfume yourself to come up here and engage in a literary discussion?" he asked.

"It's onions," said Freddy. "And I wanted to ask you—"

"Onions!" Uncle Solomon exclaimed, and tittered sarcastically. "No onion that ever grew —no, not the rankest of its species, ever could knock a grown owl off his perch at thirty yards. Yet this onion, with which you have apparently anointed yourself, very nearly did just that at a hundred, as you approached. And now will you kindly absent yourself? And downwind, if you please." His chilly little laugh rippled out again.

"Oh, for goodness' sake!" Freddy exclaimed. "Sure, I smell of onions. Spoiled onions. I got 'em to use against the rats. Now if you've had your fun, will you listen to what I have to say?"

"Been listening," said Whibley. "All we heard was quotations from Shakespeare. Very interesting. Happy to know you have literary tastes. But why not go home and read your Shakespeare instead of coming here and smelling up the woods?"

"The rats are raiding Mr. Bean's corn tonight," Freddy said. "Simon will probably lead them. If we can capture him—"

"You propose to smother him in onions?" the screech owl asked. "An excellent idea. I shall be happy to assist. Eh, Whibley?"

"We'll be up at the cornfield," Old Whibley said. "Well, what you waiting for? Promised, didn't we? Go on, take that smell out of these woods."

CHAPTER

20

So the skunks cut up the ten bags of onions with knives which Freddy had borrowed from Mrs. Bean. They cut them into quarters and put them back in the bags. But even for them it was a terrible job, and for it, later, the whole family was awarded the Benjamin Bean Distinguished Service Medal. For three of the younger ones were overcome and had to be given artificial respiration to bring them to, and all the others felt queer for weeks afterward. They smelt queer, too.

Then ropes were attached to the bags and when the spies brought word that the rats had left on their raid, all the larger farm animals hauled them up to the Grimby house and dumped them down into the cellar. When the rats came back after a couple of hours, they were laughing and singing. And Simon was with them. For he was a wise old rat, and although he didn't know how closely the A.B.I. watched all his activities, he did know that he was being spied on. And so at the last moment he changed his plan of campaign, and instead of going to the cornfield they went in the other direction and pulled up an acre of young cabbage plants. And Mr. Pomeroy did not learn of this in time to tell the owls, who were patiently watching an empty cornfield.

The rats were making a good deal of noise as they came home, but as they approached their cellar, and the dreadful smell of spoiled onions crept into their noses, they became quieter. When at last they found that they were unable to get into the cellar at all, and that the holes and runs which they had dug, and where they had stored their provisions, were closed to them, they were good and mad. They milled around on the windward side of the cellar, and

occasionally one would make a quick dash at
the steps, only to be brought up short when that
terrible smell rolled to meet him.

Rats are vicious and bad tempered animals,
particularly when they are hungry, and these
rats, cut off from their food supply, probably
felt a lot hungrier than they were. And pretty
soon they began fighting among themselves.
Simon, with the help of Ezra, broke up several
of these fights; and then he cuffed and slapped
his rioting family into silence.

"Listen to me," he said. "There's no good
standing around and yelling. This cellar is no
use any more; it will be a year before any of us
can go in there, and in any case all the food is
so tainted with rotten onions that we couldn't
eat it. We have got to give up the Grimby house.

"But that isn't to say that we are going to
give up in our fight against Freddy and his
gang. We're going to go back in the woods and
dig in. We're going to keep up our raids, and
we'll fight this fight to a decision this time. Old
Bean and his smart pig and his educated cows
and the rest of 'em—they'll be sorry before
we're through with them. We'll take the farm
this time.

"But there are things to do. Eli, you go get
Garble. He's probably at the Underdunk house
in Centerboro. It'll take you till morning, and

by that time whoever drove us out of the cellar with these onions will show up here, probably with guns. Garble must get the police here. He must tell them that Ben Bean's rocket ship is on his property, and that they have got to make him remove it. That will get the police here; then if the Bean animals come, we can have them arrested for trespassing.

"The rest of you come with me. That ship is fully provisioned, and what we have got to have first, now that our food supply is spoiled, is provisions."

The rocket was indeed almost ready for its next flight, and Uncle Ben had enough food for several months stored in it. He never bothered to close the door. The ladder gave the rats some trouble, but, once up it, they soon broke into the food lockers.

It was at about this time that Old Whibley and Uncle Solomon, having waited in vain for several hours at the cornfield, flew back to the Big Woods to see what had happened. The rats had just broken open a box containing a dozen large fruit cakes, and were laughing and shouting and having a gay old time. The owls looked at each other. They didn't say anything. Then Whibley flew up and perched on the tip of the rocket and stood poised there, ready to swoop if a rat poked his nose out of the door; and Uncle

Solomon flew off to warn Freddy of what had happened.

Inside of an hour the army of the F.A.R. had been mobilized. Ten minutes later it marched. For fighting the rats in the open, the high command felt, was different from fighting them in a dark cellar. With his flanks exposed, and no holes to dodge into, Simon could be fought on at least equal terms.

Mrs. Wiggins, as President and Commander-in-chief, led. Beside her went Hank, his rheumatism forgotten, proudly carrying the flag, and just behind marched her staff: Freddy, Jinx and Charles, with Leo, representing the circus. And then the animals: the two cows, Mrs. Wiggins's sisters; Peter, the bear; Mac, the Wildcat; Bill, the goat; Freddy's horse, Cy; the two dogs; the fox; and then all the small animals—woodchucks and skunks and squirrels and chipmunks and rabbits, two by two—a most imposing procession. Even the two ducks, Alice and Emma, waddled along determinedly in the rear.

At the edge of the Big Woods the army spread out and continued the advance on a broad front. As they moved up through the trees, they could hear the singing and shouting as the rats caroused in the storage room of the space ship. The order was passed down the line: "Advance quietly. The signal for the charge

will be given by the bugle." Jinx, of course, was
the bugle; he could lift his voice in a wail that
carried half a mile, and had indeed once spent
some time practicing bugle calls. But he had
never become very good at them. Cats are per-
sistent enough when waiting for something to
eat to come out of a mouse hole, but they won't
keep up practicing singing, or playing any instrument, unless they get rewarded all the time.

But the charge was never sounded, for as the
army closed in on the rocket it became obvious
that there was nothing to charge at. The ship
was an impregnable fortress. Mrs. Wiggins
consulted with her staff, and then Jinx went
forward under a flag of truce to demand surrender.

The rats laughed and sang louder than ever,
and the songs they sang were not complimen-
tary.

"Freddy, Freddy, Snoopy-snoot!
Wears the farmer's cast-off suit.
See the pig in farmer's clothing;
Look on him, O rats, with loathing.
Dirty Freddy, dirty suit.
Snoopy, sneaky, piggy-snoot!

Dirty old Freddy!
When he goes to bed, he
*   Keeps on his breeches and keeps on his shoes.*

Keeps on his shirt—he
Likes *to be dirty;*
  *Never washes, swims, scrubs, bathes, or
                                 shampoos.*"

The rats refused to listen to Jinx, and finally he returned to where Mrs. Wiggins and her staff were waiting.

"Well," she said, "I guess we'll have to settle down to a siege. If we surround 'em, at least we can keep 'em from getting out and doing any more damage. And they'll have to come out sometime. They've got lots of food, but the water tanks aren't filled yet. They'll get pretty thirsty by tomorrow."

"Hey," said Freddy suddenly, "they're monkeying with the fuel control valves!" He ran out and stood under the door of the ship, which was still open. "Hey, Simon!" he called. "You better leave all those levers and valves alone, or first thing you know you'll be sailing around above the stratosphere."

Loud jeers were all that answered him, and he came back. "We've just got to hope," he said, "that they don't pull the wrong levers. The ship's all ready to go. But I don't know what we can do."

"I've been wondering," said Mrs. Wiggins,

"if we oughtn't to send for the Martians. Maybe they'd be some help."

"I don't think so," Freddy said. "Webb tells me that they're very peaceable people—the kind that like to sit around on the sidelines and cheer, but don't particularly want to get into the fight."

"Well, there's nothing much to cheer about now," Leo remarked.

But the siege didn't last long. About eight in the morning four people came out into the clearing around the rocket: Mrs. Underdunk, Mr. Garble, and two state troopers. The rats became suddenly quiet.

"This the ship you want Ben Bean to move?" one of the troopers asked. "Well, I'll go down to the farm and tell him to get it out of here. Though how he's going to do it—"

"That's his problem," said Mr. Garble. "What are you animals doing here?" he asked Mrs. Wiggins. "This is my property; you'll have to get out."

"Bean's animals, ain't they?" said the other trooper. "Sure, you're Freddy, aren't you? Well, Freddy, you'll have to leave—you and your friends. Good grief, how many of you are there?"

"Couple of hundred," said Freddy. "And we're here to—"

"I don't care what you're here for!" Mr. Garble exclaimed angrily. Now get out, or I'll have you all run in."

"Guess you'd better do as he says," said the trooper. "It's his land—"

"Hey, look," said Freddy. "You promised that Uncle Ben could keep the rocket here. And he'll be ready to start out in it in a day or two more."

"You blackmailed me into promising," Mr. Garble replied. "You were going to tell Boomschmidt that the Martians weren't real. But there aren't any fake Martians any more. So I guess he'll have to take his machine out of here. And you get out too, all of you. What's that?" he asked, as his sister whispered in his ear. "Oh, well, I don't see why not. It's just Simon in there."

Mrs. Underdunk started towards the rocket. The first trooper said: "What's all this? Who's in there?"

"Workmen," said Mr. Garble. "My sister just wants to have a peek inside."

They watched her as she crossed the open space before the ship. She went up the ladder and stepped inside. And then Freddy heard a noise that he recognized—the squeak of the valve that controlled the fuel, and the little plop that fired the burner that set off the rocket.

WHOOSH! the ship shot up into the sky.

"Stand back!" he yelled. "They've started her! Run!" And he threw himself flat on the ground.

Fortunately, they were all standing back at a considerable distance. For suddenly, with a terrific roar, flame burst from the lower end of the rocket, and then with a tremendous *Whoosh!* the ship shot up into the sky. Trailing smoke and flame, it gathered speed, the roar died away; in a matter of seconds it was out of sight.

"Gosh, and they had the door open!" Jinx exclaimed, as he picked himself out of a bush into which the blast had blown him.

"It closes automatically when the ship starts," Freddy said. "But oh, golly, what will Uncle Ben say?"

CHAPTER

21

Zeke and the four other rats were getting pretty sick of their prison. It was a large rat-trap, but it had never been intended to accommodate so many guests. It was rather like a sardine can with open sides. Another bad feature was that the rat named Banjo snored. As there was nothing for them to do but sleep, since they were packed so tightly they couldn't even do setting-up exercises, this was very trying, and so they did their best to keep Banjo awake. They bit him till he squealed.

They squabbled so much that Willy got pretty tired of having them in his cage, and it was on the morning that Mrs. Underdunk and Simon and his family had sailed off into the solar system that the boa decided to do something about it. He couldn't appeal to Mr. Boomschmidt, who had never known that Mr. Garble's Martians were fakes, so he started off for the Bean farm, to see Freddy.

He was just gliding down Main Street in Centerboro when he heard a sound of singing, and then the shuffle and tramp of many feet, and around the corner came the entire army of the F.A.R., with banners flying, singing at the top of their lungs. It was a new marching song Freddy had composed. The verse was to the tune of "The Battle Hymn of the Republic," and the chorus to "Tramp, Tramp, Tramp, the Boys Are Marching."

"On, the starry flag is flying, and the summons has been sent,
And the animals are rallying around their President;

When the Bean farm is in danger, none can be
   indifferent,
      So we march to victory!

CHORUS

Tramp, tramp, the animals are marching!
Look out, Simon, here we come!
   For beneath the starry flag
   (Though we do not like to brag)
We will bang you on the nose until it's numb!

You can hear our bugles blowing, you can hear
   the steady beat
Of our drums, and now the shuffle of a thousand
   marching feet;
And you'd better pack your suitcases and gallop
   up the street,
      For we march to victory!"

There was another verse, but Freddy hadn't finished it, so it had to be sung like this:

"You can rum ti tum ti tumty, As we dum di
   dum di doe.
We've prepared for you a tumty that will fill
   you full of woe.
We will dum di dum di dum you till you dum
   di dum di doe,
      As we march to victory!"

Of course a lot of people sing "The Star Spangled Banner" that way.

Their purpose, however, was far from warlike. When their enemy had vanished into the sky, there suddenly wasn't anything for them to do. An army which has marched to the attack, and then finds that there isn't anything to attack, looks pretty foolish. So they had decided to go to the circus. They had marched all the way from the farm.

And Mr. Garble was with them. He was not, however, a prisoner—at least he was a willing prisoner—he had come along at Freddy's suggestion in the hope that he might be able to persuade the Martians to do something to rescue his sister.

Mr. Garble was not fond of his sister. He was not fond of anybody but Mr. Garble. But he didn't want to lose her, because he lived on an allowance that she gave him, and if she was careering around somewhere in the Milky Way, who was going to sign his checks?

Inside the circus grounds the army broke ranks and went to look at the side shows. Mr. Garble, with Freddy and Leo—and, of course, Mr. Webb—went to the Martian tent, where Mrs. Peppercorn was taking in the half-dollars. He started to dip a hand into the barrel, but Mrs. Peppercorn rapped him sharply across the wrist. "You keep your sticky fingers out of there, young Herbert," she said. "I don't know who this money belongs to now, but certainly none of it belongs to you."

He started to protest, but a deep voice interrupted. "Muster Garble. I been lookin' for yuh. That there joke yuh tol' me—wull now, wull you just tell it to me again?"

"There's no time now, Herc," Mr. Garble said impatiently. "I'm busy." He started to go into the tent.

But Mr. Hercules took him by the arm. "Only take a minute," he said. "Look now, Muster Garble. Mike says to Pat: 'Begorry'—no, that ain't it—'Begorra'—that's how 'twas—'Begorra, Pat, 'tis a foine day.' That right, Muster Garble?"

"Sure, sure," said the other. "And now, let's—"

"Then Pat says: 'Sure, if it don't rain.' That the way 'twas, Muster Garble?"

"You've got it exactly right, Herc," Mr. Garble replied. "Ouch, don't squeeze my arm so hard."

"Uh thought that's way 'twas," said Mr. Hercules. "But Uh been trying to laugh about it, because you said 'twas funny. Been tryin' hard, Muster Garble. But Uh couldn't. So Uh told ut to 'Restes. He says 'tain't funny. Thut wasn't nice, Muster Garble, tellin' me 'twas funny when 'twasn't. 'Twasn't nice at all."

Mr. Garble laughed. "Just a joke, Herc. Just a joke."

"Yuh. But Muster Garble, when Uh get fixed to laugh, Uh got to laugh. U'm all fixed now, and nothin' to laugh at. So I got to make somethin', ain't I?"

"Sure, Herc; sure."

"O.K.," said Mr. Hercules. "U'm goin' to warm your breeches, Muster Garble." So he grabbed Mr. Garble and turned him over his knee and gave him a good sound spanking.

Mr. Garble howled and roared with pain and anger, and Mr. Hercules howled and roared with laughter, and I don't know which made the most noise. A lot of animals and people gathered. Most of them laughed, too, for Mr. Garble was as unpopular a character as you could find in the entire county. But Andrew, the hippo, said:

"Aw, let him up, Herc, you're hurting him."

"Think so?" said Mr. Hercules. He turned Mr. Garble the other way up as easily as though he were a doll, and looked in his face. "Huh!" he said. "Face is red. But it ain't his face I'm spankin'." Then he began laughing again and set Mr. Garble on his feet. And Mr.

Garble hurried away, rubbing his back with both hands.

Freddy went on into the tent, and with the help of Mr. Webb had a talk with Two-clicks. The Martian said he'd be glad to go after Uncle Ben's ship with the flying saucer. "We can overtake her all right," he said, "and we can transship the passengers without harming them. But we can't bring the rocket back again."

So Freddy arranged with him to catch the rocket, and then to take Mrs. Underdunk and the rats out to Mr. Orville P. Garble, in Montana. "He'll probably pay her fare home," Freddy said, "just as he did Mr. Garble's. But he won't send the rats home. And I guess we'll be rid of them for good."

"How about having the saucer take those rats in the trap in my cage along?" Willy asked. "I'm kind of sick of 'em, to tell you the truth. Snarl and snap and squabble twenty-five hours a day."

So the Martians agreed to that, too. Because, they said, the animals had been very nice to them, and anyway, they liked earth. They'd like to stay on it for a while. Only not in a cage. Maybe Freddy could arrange that. They'd just as soon be in the circus—march in the parade, and even have Mr. Hercules do a juggling act

with them. Possibly they could give people
rides in the flying saucer at so much a head.
They'd split what they took in with Mr.
Boomschmidt, but they would like to earn a lit-
tle money while they were on earth. What did
Freddy think of that?

Freddy thought it was wonderful, and when
Mr. Boomschmidt was told of it he was so excited that he threw his hat on the ground and
jumped on it. "Oh, goodness!" he said. "Oh,
goodness gracious me! What an act that will
be! Eh, Leo? Ride in a flying saucer, five dollars. Ten dollars to New York and back. Trip
to the moon—golly, we could ask fifteen dollars for that, couldn't we? But just think, Leo
—a circus with real Martians! I think I ought
to take 'em into partnership, eh?"

And indeed that was what later happened.
For the Martians stayed on for nearly a year,
and in that year Boomschmidt's Stupendous &
Unexcelled Circus (Stars from Mars) made
more money than it had made in all the years it
had been on the road.

This all looked very nice at the time, but
Freddy was worried about Uncle Ben. What was
he going to do? He had spent all his money
getting his rocket ship ready for its second trip,
and now it was gone.

But Uncle Ben, not being much of a talker,

did a lot of thinking. He had been shown through the flying saucer and had ridden in it, and instead of talking about what he saw, he thought about it.

Later he had a number of conversations in sign language with the Martians. And the result was that in order to study the saucer more closely he traveled that summer with the circus, paying his expenses by giving people rides at a dollar a head in his atomic-powered station wagon. People who couldn't afford the five dollars for the saucer ride, or who were afraid of the Martian chauffeur, were eager to ride in the first car ever to use an atomic engine.

It was not a comfortable ride, for Uncle Ben had never succeeded in completely controlling the tremendous power of the engine, and sometimes, when too much power suddenly developed, the rickety old station wagon would practically gallop, and once or twice it left the ground entirely and sailed through the air for thirty or forty yards. This didn't matter so much in the country, but it was troublesome in city driving.

So Uncle Ben didn't much mind the loss of his space ship, for he was more interested in building a ship that could get to Mars than in actually getting there himself. And when the Martians offered to take him there in their

The Martians overtook them somewhere northeast of Saturn.

saucer, he said no, thank you kindly. And began to build a saucer of his own.

A week or so after Mrs. Underdunk and the rats flew off into the sky, the Martians overtook them, somewhere northeast of Saturn. Lacking Uncle Ben's know-how, they had steered in the wrong direction, and were nearly out of the solar system. Two-clicks, however, managed to lay the saucer alongside the rocket—which was something of a feat, when you consider that its speed was over a million miles a minute, while the slower rocket traveled at only a hundred thousand miles per hour. It was something of a feat, too, to transship the passengers without exploding them in the airlessness of space. But it was done, and the saucer brought them safely back to Twin Buttes, Montana. From there, Mrs. Underdunk returned to her home. As for the rats, nothing has been heard from them, and it is to be hoped that nothing will.

But you will remember that there was one rat, Eli, who did not go in the space ship. He was sent by Simon to fetch Mr. Garble to the Big Woods. But he did not return to the Big Woods with Mr. Garble. For he was hot, after his long run into Centerboro, and he stopped to get a chocolate malted before starting back. He was just too late. By the time he got back to the Big Woods the rocket had vanished into the sky. What became of him after that it is too early to know. No doubt, however, that he will be heard from again.

Freddy was pretty well satisfied with the way things had turned out. The rats had gone, and this time, he thought, for good. There had been no battle. At present, Freddy has taken up the study of the Martian language, and has already written one poem in that difficult tongue. Unfortunately, it is not possible to print it. Written Martian looks a good deal as if a duck had stepped into a pool of ink and then walked across the paper. And you could not, of course, understand it. Instead, we will end with a song which Freddy wrote while he was shut up in the crate in Mrs. Humphrey Underdunk's cellar. Your true poet will make his verses, no matter how painful his life may be. In prison, or tied to the stake with the savages dancing about him in a yelling circle—still he will sing. At least that is what Freddy said. He admitted privately, however, that he couldn't compose poetry when he had a stomach-ache.

This is what he wrote:

"A high-spirited person like me
Who has always been active and free
When confined in a crate

Does not shout: 'This is great!'
And indulge in mirth, laughter, and glee.

"On the other hand, though I don't care
To give myself up to despair,
*   To bellow and roar,*
*   And to dance on the floor,*
And by handfuls to tear out my hair,

"Yet it's hard to be feeling courageous
When faced with a fate so outrageous;
*   To be placed on a spot*
*   Which is bound to be hot,*
And decidedly disadvantageous.

"Fate's decided—and nothing can change her—
That I must be faced with the danger
*   Of being chopped up*
*   An eaten for sup-*
per by probably some perfect stranger!

"I can't help it. I'm shiverin' and shakin'
For my heart it is almost a-breakin'
*   To think the last round-up*
*   Will find me all ground up*
As sausage, or turned into bacon.

"So no wonder my teeth start to chatter,
Yet if I'm to appear on a platter,

I'll sure do my best
To smile at the guests;
And when carved, I will try not to spatter."

Freddy called his song "From Crate to Plate." So maybe he wasn't so terribly scared after all.

A NOTE ON THE TYPE

The text of this book was set on the Linotype in Baskerville. Linotype Baskerville is a facsimile cutting from type cast from the original matrices of a face designed by John Baskerville. The original face was the forerunner of the "modern" group of type faces.

John Baskerville (1706-75), of Birmingham, England, a writing-master, with a special renown for cutting inscriptions in stone, began experimenting about 1750 with punch-cutting and making typographical material. It was not until 1757 that he published his first work. His types, at first criticized, in time were recognized as both distinct and elegant, and his types as well as his printing were greatly admired.